W. Watman Smith

An Imaginary Dialogue

With Other Poems

W. Watman Smith

An Imaginary Dialogue
With Other Poems

ISBN/EAN: 9783337158422

Printed in Europe, USA, Canada, Australia, Japan

Cover: Foto ©Andreas Hilbeck / pixelio.de

More available books at **www.hansebooks.com**

AN

IMAGINARY DIALOGUE.

WITH

OTHER POEMS.

BY

W. WATMAN SMITH.

LONDON:

TRÜBNER & CO., PATERNOSTER ROW.

1873.

INDEX.

iv

PREFACE.

THE principal poem in this volume opens with the two celebrated travellers Belzoni and Burckhardt entering the catacombs of ancient Egypt by the sacred way, to make discoveries and view the remains of mummies which had been walled up for three thousand years. Selecting one of the mummies from the heap, the imaginary dialogue is carried on by the three speakers of the piece, who relieve each other in turn and help to impart interest to the historical narrative down to the period of Egyptian rule and pre-eminence, when domestic life is em-bodied, until luxury and extravagance hastened her downfal and proved her ruin. The private history of the mummy is then disclosed from her childhood, including her amatory passion, which occasioned her mental illness and removal to a lunatic asylum, from which she was liberated by the lunacy commissioners. She exposes the heartless villany of her uncle. The details of her subsequent career, with her conjugal unhappiness, prompted her to plot the tragic end of her husband, which shortly after led her to commit suicide.

The "Pictorial Sea Views" include some of the chief incidents of ocean life, and possess an interest more or less in unison with the subjects illustrated. Those here exhibited will be most familiarly recognized by all who have crossed the flood of waters, and witnessed some of the pictures here exhibited. The dull monotony of sea and sky in a long voyage must necessarily be barren of events, compared to the land, which is so fruitful of incidents, both in number and variety, that they almost require an apology for their introduction here.

"Dreamland" is a fanciful assemblage of ideal images therein described; we scale the loftiest mountain, and search around for the infinite and

sublime, as depicted by astronomers and poets, and
above these clustering stars we assign a local habit-
ation to immortal spirits, about whom we lingering
dream, glancing as we proceed at fairyland and the
Elysian fields. Thence the soul descends into the
crater of a volcano to the river Styx, where old
Charon plies his trade for human freight, with which
he crosses to the spectral shore, where a view is
obtained of the court and judges who are trying the
guilty at the bar of justice. A feeble attempt to
describe Hell, with its awful scenes of misery, is
brought to a conclusion at dawn of day by awakening to consciousness and the crow of chanticleer.

A general description of " The Flood" in all its
varied phases is here attempted to be sketched, and
ships, castles, palaces, bridges, cathedrals, theatres,
monuments, cities, etc., are overwhelmed and extin-
guished from the map of the world : the isles first
disappear beneath the surging billows, and after that
a general invasion of the deep spreads to the conti-
nental shores, utterly destroying and swallowing up

not only all animal and vegetable life, but the industrial works of man.

Some sought safety in flight and immigrated to the new world of America, and settling down in different localities in time raised new colonies at our antipodes and spread the Anglo-Saxon race far and wide, until the new country promises ere long to eclipse the old one.

AN

IMAGINARY DIALOGUE,

BETWEEN

BELZONI, BURCKHARDT, AND AN
EGYPTIAN MUMMY.

.

B

IMAGINARY DIALOGUE.

Scene: the entrance to the Catacombs of Egypt,
by the Sacred Way.

DARK, cavernous, and underground
A solemn stillness reigns around:
Long corridors and galleries led
To wall'd up chambers of the dead;
Where they in cold oblivion rot
Without distinction, and forgot,
In subterranean vaults where lie
The ashes of mortality,
For generations long pass'd by;
It may be rich and nobly born,
Or humbly poor in rags forlorn;

Here starless broods perpetual night,
Seen by a flambeau's glimmering light;
Where particles of dust arise
As we grope through, and blind our eyes:
The stifling atmosphere provokes,
And irritable trachea chokes.
A gas escape,—a charnel smell,
Issues from those once loved so well;
And echoes of the softest sound
Reverberate through crypts around.

PART I.

Bel. WHOM have we found reposing here
In such strange guise and swaddling gear?
Embalmed and wrapt in serecloth round,
And after many ages found
Within a bone-dust catacomb,
A stone sarcophagus her tomb?
Enclosed in hieroglyphic case,
With characters of form and face.
A scroll of papyrus at her side,

Her name and lineage decide,

With age and date, and where she died.

Mum. Fie! strangers, why disturb the dead?

This sacrilege lies on your head.

Burck. Dear lady, we for pardon crave,

For this intrusion on your grave;

But we are curious to know

Who slumber in these tombs below.

Mum. 'Twas yesterday that I expired,

And from the world's vain pomp retired:

To-day like robbers you appear

To filch my trinkets buried here.

Bel. Nay, Madam! we are not so base,

Our name and country to disgrace.

Pardon my boldness, but you seem

Like one awakening from a dream,

Forgetful of th' oblivious past,

Between your era and our last:

Above three thousand years have fled

Since you were number'd with the dead.

Mum. Three thousand years! it cannot be:

Impostors, you're deceiving me;

Our annals since Man first appears

On Earth, span not four thousand years.

Bel. When you were young, ere Egypt's fall,
　　The Medes and Persians conquer'd all
　　Ancient Assyria gave birth
　　To crowded cities of the earth,
　　When Babylon was great in name
　　And Nineveh of equal fame;
　　Their grand magnificence outshone
　　All cities ever gazed upon,
　　Except in Egypt's fertile land,
　　A paragon sublime and grand !
　　King Cyrus Babylon o'erthrew,
　　And like Cambyses, Egypt too.
　　Illustrious and enlighten'd Greece
　　Renown'd for valour, arts and peace,
　　From infant states expanded grew,
　　When Sparta first dawn'd into view,
　　And classic Athens famed for laws,
　　Ennobling arts, and hostile wars,
　　Combin'd their armies to expel
　　Darius who inglorious fell;
　　And Xerxes with two million men
　　Who left their bones to bleach the plain.
　　Great Alexander then unfurl'd
　　His banner over half the world,

Subduing Persia in her pride
And Hindustan to Ganges' tide.
Then left his name upon your shore
Where the proud Pharaohs reign'd before.
He was succeeded by a train
Of Ptolemies who ages reign,
Till Cleopatra shared the throne
But after claimed it for her own;
Renown'd for elegance and grace,
And last of the Egyptian race.
Imperial Rome next trod the stage
And vanquish'd insolent Carthage,
Besieg'd Jerusalem the proud
And her apostate people bowed.
All in their turn have pass'd away
Like mammoths of a former day,
With orators and bards inspired,
Philosophers and kings admired.

Mum.   Like Janus you look aft and fore
Upon a visionary shore,
And bridge a gulf 'tween time and space,
All swarming with the human race;
These legends of the mystic kind,
Are dreams of your delusive mind.

Burck. They are not fancies of the mind,
　　　But ancient records left behind,
　　　Preserved in scrolls or handed down
　　　Traditionary from sire to son ;
　　　Or chronicled in History's page
　　　And sacred held from age to age.
　　　Though once in tow'ring height sublime,
　　　These empires are the wrecks of time.
Mum. I feel bewilder'd in a maze,
　　　As you the magic curtain raise,
　　　And in a panoramic view,
　　　Present the old world to the new ;
　　　The flight of ages seems to be
　　　Mere seconds of Eternity !
　　　My curiosity you raise,
　　　So prithee haste to modern days.
Bel. The conquering arms of Rome subdued
　　　The fierce, uncivilised and rude,
　　　Who dwelt beyond the Alpine chain,
　　　Which Cæsar cross'd in his campaign
　　　To Germany and infant Gaul,
　　　Who then were wild barbarians all :
　　　Subdued by sword and ravages,
　　　Those hostile tribes of savages.

Then pass'd in galleys to the shore
Of Britain's isle unknown before,
Encounter'd by the Ocean's tide,
And warriors bold who him defied :
Who dispute every inch of ground,
Themselves the fort which foes surround.
Who feels not proud in heart and head
When one's own kindred fought and bled
For freedom, constitution, law,
And all that is worth fighting for ?
Who would not for his country die,
Wife, children, home and liberty,
When the invader scales the walls
And at your gates in thunder calls ?

Mum.   Oracular you seem to me,
Prefiguring the world's history.
But who, and what, and whence art thou ?
A priest or Arab sheik I trow,
With turban'd shawl coil'd round thy head,
And sash and mantle o'er thee spread.

Bel.   I am a pilgrim in disguise,
And not the vagrant you surmise,
I owe my birth and honour'd name
To Padua's city, whence I came.

Wealth, pleasure, indolence and vice
Effeminate, debauch, entice,
And bring on premature decay;
Voluptuous Persia shrinks away,
With sensual Babylon the proud,
And Nineveh in her white shroud,
And pagan Rome amongst the crowd;
When Goths and Vandals from afar,
Invade with desolating war,
And struck the last decisive blow,
That laid the Empress city low,
With others famed and nobly born,
Into oblivion sunk and gone.

Mum.   From his world's entrance to the grave,
Man is a tyrant and a slave,
And restless roams his kind to slay,
Like herds of beasts or birds of prey.
The life of nations as of man,
Appears contracted to a span;
They rise to eminence to-day,
To-morrow fall and waste away,
Then into non-existence glide,
With all their conquests, wealth and pride!

Burck.   After a long forgotten past,
In which its infancy was cast,

And northern tribes its shores invade,
For pillage, conquest, war, or trade,
Benighted Europe from her dream
Awakened like the morning beam,
Struggling for freedom in her chains,
Where universal chaos reigns;
Which threw a lustre round her name,
When climbing up the hill of fame;
As in the mediæval age,
When eastern crusades were the rage,
And the crusaders fought and bled,
With Cœur-de-Leon at their head.
Enlighten'd, civilised and free,
She grew in power o'er land and sea;
And in discoveries open'd wide
Another continent, beside
Australia, China, and Japan,
Peopled with different types of man.

Mum. You sketch the world in embryo,
But of its truth I nothing know;
What you reveal and briefly tell,
O'er my mute senses casts a spell,
And the pictorial changes seem,
The shadowy figures of a dream,

Which play their part upon the stage,
In characters from age to age,
Then waste away and disappear
Like pilgrims from this lower sphere;
Leaving their tumuli on shore,
Where they encamped long time before.
But what of my dear native land?
Has her time-glass run out its sand,
Sharing the common lot of all,
In her foredoom'd decline and fall?

Burch.   A Roman province she became,
Stripp'd of her prestige, power and fame;
Until the Cæsars' broken line
Began to fade in deep decline,
And their protectorate to withdraw,
Distracted with domestic war.
Alas! she was the spoil and prey
Of conquerors in later day;
The Caliphs next in rule succeed,
A strange and Saracenic breed,
Whose wars and powerful arms reduced,
And Islamism introduced;—
Whose civil wars to flames consign'd
The intellectual wealth of mind,*

*Alexandrian Library.

Collected in that archive store
Which all the civilised deplore.

Mum. Her fate, alas! demands a tear
From those Egyptian mummies here
Who like myself her grandeur knew,
And of her fame partakers too.
Shrouded in darkness was her birth,
Though since the most renown'd of Earth
(Dispersed perchance from Babel's tower,
Attempting reachless heaven to soar).
For manufacturing works of art
And skilful industry the mart:
Her foreign commerce, arms, and trade,
Threw other nations into shade.

Burch. From Hebrew chronicles we trace
The old traditions of thy race,
When Egypt's tyranny oppress'd,
And drove them from their place of rest;
Shoots of a patriarchal line,
From Abram's sire in Palestine,
Whence sprung Prince Joseph (Jacob's son),
Who Pharaoh's confidence had won.
Who rose to fortune, power and fame,
And Egypt ruled in Pharaoh's name;

A famine them to Egypt took,
And Canaan's city they forsook.

This unalloyed and dark eyed race,
With venerable bearded face,
Bond-slaves became in servitude,
Bow'd down in spirit and subdued:
Employ'd in every menial trade,
Which worst of criminals degrade,
On pyramids and works of State,
On private mansions of the great,
Or chain'd in gangs to laden cars,
And scourged with whips that left their scars.
Their Lawgiver by mystic art
Reveal'd the secrets of God's heart,
And their deliverance did foreshow,
But Pharaoh would not let them go,
Till plagued with every earthly ill,
By magic art or miracle,
At last consented, and pursued
To the Red Sea the multitude.
The tide receded from the shore,
And let the panic-struck pass o'er,
Then back reflow'd to its own source,
Engulfing all th' Egyptian force!

Like Arabs in the wilderness,
They wander'd forth in bitterness,
Ere they before the promised land
Of Canaan on the Jordan stand!
Which honey, milk or wine o'erflows
With perfume of the atta rose;
But where they raised up border foes.
There these marauders broke the law,
And plunged in deadly strife and war
With all the petty tribes around,
And next in Babylon were found,
By Cyrus who this people free
From galling chains and slavery.
Back to Jerusalem they pour,
Their sacred Temple to restore.
Vast, lofty, ornamental, grand,
All column'd round and nobly plann'd,
With taste and elegance combin'd,
Inspired by an exalted mind,
Where was preserved the Ark of God,
His presumed spiritual abode;
Till they provoke the wrath of Rome,
And their encircling walls thrown down!
Then scatter'd wide through every land,
Cursed with th' Almighty's awful brand!

Mum. Ah! sir, my country you recall,
Its rise and progress,—pride and fall;
When in true royal grandeur, great,
She ruled the world in regal state.
Such were her laurels and her fame,
Wisdom and learning, power and name,
That sovereigns of high renown,
Paid homage to th' Egyptian crown;
Besides ambassadors of state,
Philosophers and nobles great;
Her wealth and beauty fill'd the east,
Attracting merchant, traveller, priest!

Bel. Your country elevates,—inspires,
And fills with rapturous desires:
We look amazed as we behold
Her classic taste and genius bold,
Her sacred temples,—marble halls,—
Her venerable moss-grown walls,
And altars that were wont to blaze
With sacrifice to Ammon's praise!
Long avenues of sphinxes guard
The propylæa to the façade,
With lions of majestic size,
Imperial look, and rolling eyes;

With compound figures, centaur-like,
Half man, half beast, with terror strike;
Emblems of dignity and power,
Reposing calmly in their tower
Of strength, and place, and royalty,
Guarding the Temple's Deity!
Where pillar'd porticoes arise,
And cornices of noble size,
To formal ceremonies bound,
The tabernacle's holy ground.
Grim idols here arrest the eye,
And symbolise the Deity,
Whose local dwelling is a shrine
All holy, mystic, and divine;
Where rays of light descending through,
The Holy Spirit peers in view,
Presiding o'er the Earth and Skies,
The Mystery of all mysteries!—
The God of gods, whose form unknown
Is veil'd in fancies of our own;—
The Light of lights,—the Soul of souls,
Whose Will the universe controls.
In silent reverence devotees
Fall down and worship on their knees,

C

Where Thoth! Osiris! Isis! stand
In figurative emblems grand!

Mum. Their inspired books and records old,
Staff, crosiers, flagons, cups of gold,
And mitres, candlesticks, and dress,
Were look'd on with all sacredness,
And kept in a reliquary,
With relics of antiquity,
And th' insignia, robes, attire,
Of High Priests and attendant choir.
Young choristers their praises sang,
And round the roof their echos rang,
Their hallowed mysteries were known
To their inducted priests alone.

Bel. For architectural works renown'd,
Rare specimens of art abound,
With sculptures and entablature,
And painted frescoes to allure,
Which fill with reverence and surprise
By their majestic towering size,
Exhibited in temples grand,
And palaces throughout the land.
Your obelisks and hundred gates,
Are vestiges of unknown dates;

Red granite needles rear'd on high
Are monuments to memory ;
Your antique gems,—scholastic lore,
With hieroglyphic signs of yore,
And marble statues of the great,
And public buildings of the State,
With pottery and porcelain,
And urns and vases still remain.
The mighty mausoleums stand
Memorials of a powerful land ;
Colossal Pyramids of stone,
With nothing left of dust and bone,
Which monarchs of ambitious aim,
Raised to perpetuate their fame,
And shelter in these crypt domains
Their cold inanimate remains.
These subterranean catacombs,
Division'd into cave-like rooms,
Choked up with *débris* we explore,
But fail to find the key-stone door
Of inlaid rocks upon the roof,
Or undermine the slabs in proof
Of their intended use and end :
But still these vaults an interest lend,

Though no remains are to be found,
Or mummy cases underground.

Burck. On either side the Nile we see
The remnants of antiquity.
Thebes! Memphis! Carnack! cities rare,
Look skeletons of what they were:
And On, the city of the sun,
Alas! his glorious course has run.
Pompey's pillar looks out afar,
And Memnon from his lofty car.
Where'er you tread 'tis hallow'd ground,
For everywhere are Temples found;
Fragments are scattered far and wide
On both sides the o'erflowing tide.
Edfou in ruins prostrate lies,
Despoil'd and doom'd no more to rise,
With broken columns,—granite wall,
Decay'd and nodding to their full;
The relics of Carnack you view
Admiringly as you pass through,
Mingled with feelings of regret
(A sight once seen you ne'er forget):
And tarry as you look aghast,
Reflecting on the dateless past;

The spoils of ignorance and time,
E'en now look lofty ! grand !' sublime !
  A withering canker touch of blight,
Feeds on them like a parasite,
As virulent infections seize
Upon the victims of disease,
O'ergrown with weeds, ferns, moss, and trees.
Mum. With solemn feelings you behold
An empire's dust decayed and old,
And picture the invading host
Of Alexander on the coast,
Whose ravages with fire and sword,
Spared not these Temples, but destroy'd.
Combin'd with her assistant Art,
Her helpmate Nature did her part
In gifts of myrtles, banyans, palms,
With setting sun and dazzling charms ;
In citron groves of fragrant scents,
In spices, myrrh, and frankincense,
With orchids of the rarest hue,
Whose freaks and sports attraction drew ;
Its terraced gardens,—sloping lawns,
Unruffled lakes and sheltering palms,
With crystal fountains, perfumed showers,
Reflecting the sweet tinted flowers,

And its unclouded atmosphere,
Exhilarating, bright, and clear;
Save when the dense white milky fog,
Issues from out some swampy bog;
With classic villas, snug retreats,
Stone palaces and country seats,
Stamped it a paradise of earth,
Fill'd with th' illustrious of birth.

Burck. The ocean once submerged the land,
And left its arid bed of sand,
Where gulfs between, and deserts lie,
As in historic times gone by.
Green fields now hedge the desert round,
Encompass'd by the hills that bound,
Where caravansaries are found,
And wandering Arabs scour the plain,
Where seldom falls a drop of rain;
Where dust-storms and tornadoes drive,
And camels overwhelm alive;
Where groups of girls meet at the well,
With pitchers, Eastern tales to tell.
The rock-bound cataract's awful roar,
Reverberates along the shore,

Choking the valley of the Nile,
Where lurks the weeping crocodile,
And the fleet ostrich close in land,
Buries her eggs in burning sand.

Here mosques and minarets arise,
And look aërial in the skies;
The Turks resort to the bazaar,
In Cairo or Alexandria.
The market-place for goods and ware,
Resembling Europe's fancy fair,
With noisy clamour, hue and cry,
From orientals passing by,
In varied costume of the East.
'Mid café's lounge and simple feast,
Where foreign tongues of every sound,
Are in one general hubbub drown'd.

Bel. The Ptolemies your glory raised,
And through the East your splendour blazed:
Your armies and your fleets invade,
And colonies their tribute paid;
Your steeds and charioteers appear
In mural frieze with shield and spear;
Art specimens of days gone by,
Which fill us with humility;

But no interior life they give,
Or tell how you were wont to live.

Mem. The flocks and herds on mountains feed,
The peasants reap and sow the seed,
The great to public baths repair,
To breathe the fresh ambrosial air.
The inner courtyard and arcade
Afford a cool refreshing shade
From glare and heat ; and groves of trees
Paid homage to the playful breeze.
The ladies sit in state at home,
And there receive th' *élite* who come
To garden banquet, stately ball,
Or *fête-champetre* festival.
Here chamberlains at every door,
On crimson daïs above the floor,
With golden chain and jewell'd wand,
In pageantry and court-dress stand.
The silken curtains rich and rare,
From Persian looms, keep out the glare.
Here brilliant mirrors, costly gems,
And candelabra with carved stems,
And cornices, and gilded frame,
Glass chandeliers and jets of flame,

With allegoric figures round,
And vases fill'd with flowers abound ;
With cushion'd sofas to recline,
And cabinets of rare design,
Inlaid with pearl and marquetry,
And banner screens of broidery ;
While leopard skins slung here and there
O'er ottoman and tapestry chair,
With unique model works of art,
A classic interest impart.
The thronged saloons with ladies fair,
Whose loveliness and graceful air,
With rapture fill the heart and sight,
Exhilarating with delight ;
Wore rarest ornaments of gold,
Whose dazzling splendour you behold,
Sparkling with jewel'ry as bright,
And diamonds glistening to the sight,
With emeralds of the richest dye,
And rubies shining brilliantly,
Medallion bracelets round the arm,
And necklaces of pearls to charm,
With robes of elegant work'd lace,
Disposed with fashionable grace.

The joyous company appear
Excited with the liberal cheer,
And warm into a rapturous glow,
As sparkling wit and humour flow,
Until the ladies at a sign
The gentlemen leave at their wine;
Then to the grand saloon repair,
Or open balcony's fresh air,
Where fragrant mocha's handed round,
And music echoes from the ground,
While some join in the promenade
Upon the lawn and esplanade,
To dance and listen to the song,
And chase the pleasant hours along.

Burck.   The fair sex emulous to shine
With fascinating arts divine,
In figure, beauty, and attire,
Would look the angels men admire,
Bewitching, affable, and kind,
To love and gaiety inclined.

Mum.   Retired from the meridian heat,
She seeks the boudoir's snug retreat;
A rare bijou and gem of art,
Which captivates the eye and heart;

Where festoon'd muslin curtains slung,
And water-colour drawings hung,
With reflex'd mirrors round the room,
Scented with odorous perfume.
Octagonal, the oriel light
Look'd out upon a landscape bright;
The miniature of a divan,
With cushion, couch, and ottoman,
'Mid artificial fruits and flowers,
And groups of birds in fairy bowers;
A lady's sanctum for a doze
T' enjoy the luxury of repose,
Or tête-à-tête with one or two;
As oriental ladies do.

Bel.   The artificial life you led,
O'er your luxurious kingdom spread;
To ease and comfort all incline,
Which bring on premature decline;
Pride, pleasure, indolence, entice
And lead astray to scenes of vice;
The lust of wealth, of power, and place,
Afflict with vanity the race;
Extravagance with pomp and show,
Brought ruin, death, and overthrow;

Refined, effeminate, and gay,
With ostentation and display,
Till jealous rivals you provoke,
Who all your fond delusions broke.

Mum. Professing connoisseurs of wine,
The gentlemen at home would dine,
And after to their clubs repair,
To finish with potations there ;
Indulge in gambling, billiards, dice,
And scenes of profligacy and vice ;
Slaves to their passions, loss of health,
And bankruptcy, and wasted wealth.

Alas ! this splendour passed away,
And night eclipsed her solar ray
While in my teens ; for glittering show
And envy brought patricians low,
With banquet, ball, and music room,
Which variegated lamps illume,
All aromatic with perfume,
Magnificence, indulgence, ease,
The volatile light-hearted please,
Of rank and style, and caste so proud,
So elevated 'bove the crowd.
Regardless of all costliness
They vie in fashionable dress,

Till vanity, excess, and pride,
Brought down their pomp and mortified.

PART II.

Bel. As I have sketched in brief review,
And shown the modern world to you,
Which with surprise you listened to ;
If not presumptuous thought by thee,
Reveal thy private history,
When youth was bursting into Spring,
Like buds from flowers just opening ;
When that veil'd face was lit with joy,
And happiness without alloy ;—
With light refulgent in those eyes,
Resembling the blue tinted skies,
When the mercurial spirits rise ;
When hope, and smiles, and love impart
A thrilling rapture to the heart ;
Ere a cloud floated o'er thy cheek,
A tender passion to bespeak,

Or anxious cares of wedded life,
O'ertake a mother and a wife.

Mum.   Alas! you touch a tender string,
Which agitates and leaves a sting,
That thrills my nervous system through,
As thunder shakes the volcano.
'Twere well my annals to conceal,
For what of interest can you feel
In one whose spirit pass'd away,
With myriads of a former day?
Whose chequer'd life, though reckon'd brief,
Was fill'd with melancholy grief,
Although preserved in grotesque guise,
I feel exposed to mortal eyes:
Timidity and modest fear
Steal o'er me while denuded here,
Without my robe, or such attire
The nice and delicate require;
So listen pray to my request,
And leave me in sepulchral rest;—
Its evening shade,—its still retreat,
To me are welcome! at your feet
Submissive, I now humbly bow;
Make not of me a public show,
Death wears no terrors on his brow.

Bel. Of hallow'd customs we have read,
And preservation of the dead;
'Tis hard and withering to part
With those fond treasures of the heart,
Who were our late companions here,
And next to life itself held dear;
But nature's laws brook no delay,
That which is mortal will decay,
And breed corruption day by day.
All nations exercise their skill,
Their innate instincts to fulfil,
And with becoming reverence mourn
O'er those for ever lost and gone !
Wild cannibals their dead consume,
The modern civilised entomb ;
The Parsees in the sacred way
Their corpses leave for birds of prey,
Who round the "tower of silence" herd
To feast upon the uninterr'd ;
The Greeks and Romans used to burn,
And then the sacred ashes urn.
Th' Egyptian custom as we see,
Disguised, bears no identity,
But a sad spectacle and fright,
When thus exposed to modern sight,

A wither'd, dried up, shrivell'd trunk,
Into a child's dimensions shrunk.

Mum. When in a sentimental mood,
Indulging in lone solitude,
'Twas here I used to meditate,
And mourn my parents' early fate;
To drop a pious pensive tear,
And claim the dust that's buried here;
Unconscious of Time's flowing stream,
All you describe appears a dream.
If I have slept three thousand years,
They have been without hopes or fears;
Senseless, I felt no mortal pain
Nor any wish to rise again,
Eternal slumbers us surronnd,
Without a whisper or a sound.
To you resuscitation's due,
Who sought this ghostly interview.
The laurels round their memories grace
The fame of my ancestral race.
Some heroes in the battle field,
With casque and banner, sword and shield,
Themselves distinguish'd with renown,
And honour'd service to the crown;

While some in politics were great,
And served in offices of state.
To sing their praises and admire,
Is worthy of the Muse's lyre;
But there are some I must not name,
Went branded with a mark of shame,
Whose memories were not so dear,
For they were false and insincere.

Burck. That roll of papyrus round thy arm
(Sent with thy relics to embalm),
Reveals thy parentage and name,
'Zilla' the daughter of Misraim,
And Miriam his departed wife,
Who lost her own in giving life
To the conception of her womb,
And prematurely found a tomb.
Except the date, this brief record
Is silent and breathes not a word.

Mum. 'Twere better I had ne'er been born,
Than from my mother thus be torn,
And I expired within the womb,
And shared with her a double tomb.
But Providence's wise decree,
Dealt death to her, and life to me.

D

Her transfer to the realms above,
Deprived me of her fondest love,
And strong affections of the heart,
None but a mother can impart,
With the like lineaments of face,
And gentle air, and angel grace.

   Nor this my only loss to bear,
Which left me to the fostering care
And guardianship of my poor sire,
Whose virtues would his child inspire;
His warm affection,—tender soul,
Might take her place and me control,—
His guiding precepts,—bland in tone,
Impart some graces to my own:
But stern unsympathising Fate
Pour'd down on me relentless hate,
For I was born unfortunate;
As prophesied when I was young,
By fortune-telling gipsy tongue,
Who with the oracles afar,
Held intercourse with weird and star.
My father's tears had scarcely dried,
Since that dear saint in childbirth died,
When his declining health gave way
To gnawing sorrow day by day.

He from the outer world withdrew,
Absorbed and melancholy grew,
His sinking spirits ceased to shine,
When he took on to grieve and pine,
And physically to decline.
Until he sunk to rise no more,
'Neath this dim world's receding shore!

Transferr'd into an uncle's hands,
Possessing wealth and spacious lands,
He placed me under nurse's care,
My fairy life with her to share ;
From infancy to maidenhood,
She in the room of mother stood.

Time hastened on, and with it flew
The joyous spring of childhood too,
With thoughtless mirth and laughing glee,
And fun and girlhood's mimicry,
When all our paths are lit with smiles,
And artless playfulness beguiles,
When gladd'ning sun and spirits bright
The face illume with beams of light.
When we feel neither cares nor fears,
And beauty our spring blossom cheers.

I grew and ripen'd, and in time
Youth flourish'd, and I reach'd my prime.
Those golden days hereafter gleam,
Partaking of a fairy dream,
    As up to girlhood's prime we climb,
We feel an equatorial clime
To influence our excited frame,
And passion kindle into flame.
The promptings of the human breast,
In both the sexes are confess'd,
When Cupid, with his torch and dart,
His missile hurls into your heart.
To the blind passion I confess,
With an enthusiast's happiness;
Its dreamy pictures of the mind,
And all its influences combin'd;
With the delirium of soul,
And ecstasies beyond control;
The genial smile,—the lowering frown,
That raise or cast our spirits down;
The absent mind,—the fluttering heart,
Or unkind word the tear to start;
The fond embrace,—the last adieu,
The kiss and lingering interview;

With golden promises to cheer,
And future bliss we hope to share.
Impulsively I loved at sight,
With all my heart, and soul, and might,
But could not, dared not to impart,
The padlock'd secret of my heart ;
For ancient custom quite forbade
The inclinations of a maid.   .
Admiring suitors might propose,
But guardians only could dispose.
I hugg'd the creature to my breast,
In sleepless nights of broken rest,
And on my idol mused alone,
But could not keep the passion down.
He felt not, loved not in return,
Nor knew (for aught that I could learn)
I cherish'd fondness or desire,
However much I might admire,
Though warmth of feeling will betray
The blushing damsel night and day :
I miss'd him, and 'twas whisper'd me
That he had sail'd for Italy.
No tongue could tell,—no pen could write
My feelings on that wretched night ;

It stunn'd my senses,—turn'd my brain,
I grew delirious with the pain,
And sobbed and wept the long nights through,
Which into typhoid fever threw,
And long confin'd me to my bed,
Pale, absent-minded, and half dead!

Bel. Our sympathies teach all to feel
For others' woes when they are real;
But from your plaint I apprehend
That he was but a casual friend,
Who made no vows, and gave no sign,
Profess'd no love, nor asked for thine,
But amiable, gallant, and kind,
He formed the model of your mind,
Where his reflected image shone,
And flattering charms you doted on.

Mum. Imagination on him fed
Intensely, till it turned my head,
And o'er my spirits cast a gloom
Which nothing earthly could illume:
Delusions crowded on my sight,
And God-like reason took its flight;
The balance of my mind gave way,
And there in agony I lay,

Until removed for change of air,
By fraud, a victim to despair ;—
To an asylum's dull retreat,
Which had been a manorial seat.

To my great horror and dismay,
Encompass'd, guarded, and at bay,
I found myself a prisoner there,
Placed under a physician's care ;
While some from violent restraint,
Shriek'd out, and shouted loud complaint,
And into fits of passion burst,
'Gainst their false friends, and raved and curs'd ;
While some, of melancholy mood,
Indulged ascetic solitude ;
Some with delirium tremens mad,
Look'd ghastly, wizen'd, old and sad ;
Some brooding o'er their losses sigh'd
Despairing, and like children cried;
Some were religiously insane,
Or suffer'd from a feverish brain,
Some from delusions of the mind,
Were only temporary confin'd ;
Some to prevent from suicide,
Who felt disgraced and mortified ;

And some inherited disease,
While over-study others seize ;
But most from disappointed love,
Who were as harmless as the dove.
But oh ! sad thought, some were immured
And ne'er intended to be cured,
By ravenous wolves in lambs' disguise,
Who perjuring swore on oath their lies,
For sordid purposes of gain,
And fatten'd on their victims' pain.
Such was their avarice for gold,
Certificates were bought and sold
To paid trustees and doctors' wives,
Solicitous for patients' lives.
Once through the walls and bolted gates,
You're at the mercy of the Fates,
Who rule your destiny while there,
And watch and dodge you everywhere,
And when excited, coax and calm,
Or give to keepers false alarm :
If dangerous, they with shackles bind,
And have the lunatics confined
In darken'd cells through frigid night,
And torture, terrify, affright,

With potent opiates, blister'd head,
Until exhausted and half dead ;
Your lion spirit gets subdued,
And crush'd in lonely solitude :
If only sorrowful and sad,
The brutal treatment drives you mad ;
Pretended friends and artful foes
The wretched satellites impose,
And letters you desire to post,
Are intercepted, burnt, or lost.

Burck. Your inuendo would impute
And brand with infamy the brute,
Who could such monstrous crime design,
And in a prison cell confine,
And who like birds of prey devour
The wealth of those within their power.
Madam, how long were you confined
In this half frantic state of mind?

Mum. The summer solstice thrice had run,
And wheel'd around the central sun,
Ere I was certified as well,
And loosen'd from those chains of hell,
For state commissioners inquired,
And my discharge at once required.

1 to that uncle was conveyed,
Who stood aghast, and look'd amazed,
For he ne'er cherish'd love for me
Beyond respect and courtesy,
Nor I for him ; he was so cold
And taciturn, besides a scold ;
So irritable and waspish grown,
He petrified you into stone.
Dissembler, egotist, and cheat,
In whom the worst of passions meet ;
He ne'er consulted with his niece,
Or gave consent to her release,
For I was doom'd my days to end,
Where I was snared, without a friend.

Burck.   So what with prejudice and pride,
No love was lost on either side ;
Your friendship never took firm root
Nor, budding, blossom'd into fruit,
Nor confidence possessed the heart,
Its treasured secrets to impart.

Mum.   When my dear father grew so ill,
He thought of me and made his will
In a desponding state of mind,
Which he unwitness'd seal'd and sign'd,
And from that death-knell hour declined.

To me he left all he possess'd,
And sank into oblivious rest,
Appointing two trustees by name,
Without their license for the same,
Who both renounced, and would not move
That legal instrument to prove.
The property neglected lay,
And threatened soon to melt away,
When he whom I must uncle call,
Although unprincipled withal,
Administer'd unto a will,
And its contents swore to fulfil.
My guardian governess this knew,
And pledged her solemn oath 'twas true.

Burch. At the first blush it would appear
A generous act for one so dear,
The handsome, graceful thing to do,
Which show'd an interest felt for you;
But underneath a crafty mind,
Some secret plot is oft design'd.

Mum. The narrow circle of our home
Was often into parties thrown;
A gentleman came oft to dine,
Who was a connoisseur of wine,

Chephron by name, of manners bland,
Who proved a suitor for the hand
Of my spoil'd cousin lady fair,
Whose flattering and obsequious air,
And garrulous and honied tongue,
A soft enchantment round her flung,
Appealing to her vain conceit,
By oily words, cant, and deceit,
And season'd his repeated tale
With anecdotes till they grew stale.

Bel.   The changeful moon with borrow'd light
Illumes the firmament of night,
But what's the chilling earth to one
Without the warm inspiring sun ?
Or love when not responded to,
But a bleak world with heaven in view ?
Admiring beauty in the young,
The soul enamours and the tongue,
And o'er one's sunbright spirits throw,
A wreath of glory round the brow.

Mum.   Time in his chariot round the sun,
His annual race had nearly run ;—
That sun which honour'd at their birth
The stars that lit the face of Earth ;—

That Earth which out of chaos sprung,
And as a sphere suspended hung ;
When omens dire in heaven's highway,
Gave tokens of approaching fray,
Which ere long burst o'er Mæris' head
In lightning flames and thunder spread.
For Chephron with Nydia sparr'd,
And their religious feelings jarr'd.
His faith was in one Deity,
Hers in Egyptian imagery.
Their different creeds led to dispute,
Each tried the other to confute
By suasive eloquence of speech,
And to convince or overreach.
At last indifferent they grew,
And colder at each interview ;
Till visits which had frequent been,
Were now but scant and far between,
Until that chilling word—"farewell"
Brought on her a mesmeric spell.
A sunless world, and lost to sight,
She wither'd as if struck with blight,
That like a cancer gnaws the heart,
And spreads disease through every part.

This caused her brother to complain,
And her false lover to explain,
And honour to demand redress
For injury he'd not confess :
A duel only could decide,
And satisfy their wounded pride.

Bel. A chivalrous appeal to arms
For injured love hath secret charms ;
Their high-bred spirit, rank and pride,
Are oft to royal blood allied ;
And knights and squires of high degree
Are jealous of their pedigree.
To arms ! to arms ! the hero cries,
And echo answers in replies.

Mum. Poor Amos, up at break of day,
Went with his second to the fray,
His sister's insult to avenge
(But not from malice or revenge).
The hostile combatants were found
Assembled on the chosen ground.
With foils whose cold and deadly steel,
Less brave of heart might shuddering feel.
Heroic courage fired each breast,
And skilful science put to test.

The seconds ranged on either side,
The challeng'd challenger defied,
And at a signal they began,
When fire along their rapiers ran,
The clashing strife grew hot and fierce,
Each tried the other's breast to pierce,
And louder sounds the deadly strife,
Which sought to take each other's life;
Strategic skill and self defence,
With parried thrusts provoke incense,
They first advance, and cautious meet,
Cross swords and fence, and then retreat;
Now stand at bay to breathe the air,
With flashing eyes of meteor glare.
They measure paces, close again,
And fiercer strike, but not in vain :
Chephron in warding off a blow,
Received a scratch, and blood let flow;
The lightning flash,—the thunder stroke,
Again upon the welkin broke;
Again the hostile clamour spread.
Again they aim at heart and head ;
Again the heat of battle warms,
And feebler grew their weary arms,

When Chephron made a feint, and thrust
His adversary to the dust:
The rapier enter'd at his side,
From whence gush'd forth the crimson tide;
His corpse lay weltering at their feet,
And all the dualists retreat.

Burck. But what of Mœris? did he mourn
His son's loss on that fatal morn?
Did he his daughter's fate deplore
When his boon friend return'd no more?
Did he his perfidy condemn,
Or try the angry tide to stem?
And reconcile the severed pair
With soothing words and earnest prayer?

Mum. A messenger arrived in town,
With news to strike one's spirit down,
And soon the corpse of Amos pale,
Confirmed the sad, the piteous tale.
The gaping wound, oh! ghastly sight,
Bore witness of the murd'rous fight:
We gather'd round with streaming eyes,
And felt our curdled blood to rise;
All stood transfix'd in mute despair,
And look'd on with a maniac's stare,
With mournful moans which rent the air.

In a wild paroxysm of grief
His sister Nydia found relief,
Herself accused as she hung o'er
Her brother's corpse all grimed with gore,
And her dishevell'd head-dress tore,
As she knelt down to kiss his face,
And smother in a short embrace.

Our house became a living tomb,
Darken'd and draped in sable gloom,
With household mourners passing by
In silent whisperings and deep sigh;
The drowsy lamp and bated breath
Wore the solemnity of death;
When the embalmers took away
The livid corpse which shewed decay.

Mæris, shut up in wild despair,
Abstain'd from food and tore his hair,
And looking thoughtful on the dead,
He cried for vengeance on the head
Of Chephron, who from justice fled.
Dejected, misanthropic, low,
He felt or feign'd to feel the blow,
That nipp'd the flow'ret in the bud,
The last link of ancestral blood.

Burck. When Amos' obsequies were o'er,
Whose tragic end his friends deplore,
Did Nydia deeply feel and pine,
And waste away in slow decline,
After her brother's cruel fate,
When love for Chephron turn'd to hate?
Mum. Embalming was a work of time,
The progress tedious, slow, and grime,
Resembling a dissecting room,
Which frankincense and spice perfume:
A scientific art of trade,
With costly license to be paid,
Where trust and confidence are placed,
And recognition can't be traced.
Outside the city walls the dead
In beehive catacombs are laid;
The rich sarcophagi provide,
The poor encased lie side by side.
Here the heroic Amos sleeps,
And o'er him his fond sister weeps.
Her first love's sorrow pass'd away,
Her brother's deeper rooted lay,
And settled on her pallid brow,
Which look'd a coronet of snow;

And cold to all the world was she,
Indulging in despondency.

Now rumour with its busy tongue
Throughout the capital was rung,
Official visitors inquire,
And through the streets the public crier
Denounced the homicide by name,
And reward offer'd for the same ;
This led to Chephron's arrest,
Who to the serious crime confess'd,
And pleaded guilty to the charge,
Hoping for mercy and discharge,
Extenuating his offence
For duelling in self defence,
'Twas Amos who the challenge sent,
And he deserved the punishment.

Justice and Mercy in the scales
Suspended hung ; the last prevails :
But to imprisonment and fine
The judges sentence and confine,
To satisfy the injured law,
And duellists to overawe.

Burck.   As northern lights bestrew the sky,
Dark omens like a prophecy,

Upon the occult future draw
The shadows of impending war;
So I predict, although no seer,
A thundering explosion near,
Wherein all Mæris' wrath will burst,
And from his house will Zilla thrust.

Mum. Be not surprised when I complain,
A trodden worm will turn again :
'Twas more than flesh and blood could bear
To see him rave and storm and swear,
And sullenly I left the room,
My independence to assume,
And passed a wretched sleepless night,
Until the slow return of light,
When all my grievances I wrote,
Addressed in a becoming note,
Reproving him of cruel wrong,
The weak contrasting with the strong.

An outcast with an end in view,
I visited some friends I knew,
Whom I took counsel of before,
Who were th' attornies to restore
Me to the world and liberty,
From bonds worse than captivity,

When I was treacherously beguiled,
And treated as deranged and wild.
Mœris they called a perfect bear,
And offer'd me their home to share :
Spontaneously to them I sprung,
And in each other's arms we hung.

Burck.   Which would enrage and fill with ire,
His bosom of volcanic fire.

Mum.   A dictatorial letter stern,
From Mœris summoned my return.
No longer minor, his command
Was answered with a reprimand
By the adviser of my choice,
Who threatened the law to enforce,
In case of fraud or hostile force.
That for the future I should claim
Th' estates he managed in my name ;
Demanding statement of affairs,
And settlement for twenty years.
My health restored from withering blight,
Amidst the constellation bright,
Of happy faces round me thrown,
Imparted sunshine to my own,
And o'er my broken spirits threw
A glowing warmth they seldom knew.

Convivial friends of either sex
In little evening parties mix,
The social discourse to prolong,
With lively dance and syren song,
To animate, amuse, unite,
In giving pleasure and delight.
Amongst the coterie was one,
Whom my attractive features won ;
Of swarthy race and Indian caste,
Who life's meridian long had past,
A barrister of some repute,
Who prayed me to accept his suit :
A dapper little man and trim,
With more than met the eye in him ;.
Bland, affable, polite, and gay,
With always something sweet to say ;
Who was in disposition kind,
And courteous to womankind.

PART III.

Bd. As nestling birds instinctive fly
In search of food and liberty,

Their flutt'ring wings untried before,
Will skip ere they attempt to soar;
So you forsook the satyr's den,
And like a little orphan wren,
Attracted left your uncle's home
In quest of friends, and farther roam;
The long robed gentleman to meet
A humble suppliant at your feet,
Who knew you were an heiress born
To wealth, and thus began to fawn,
So that the suitor for your hand
Was special pleader for your land.

Mum. The Nile had reached its overflow
For full two lunar months or so,
Depositing its foreign spoil
On Egypt's rich alluvial soil,
Till it had reach'd its annual height,
Then ebbed and vanish'd out of sight;
So Zenos like that noble stream
Advanced to favour and esteem,
Though I retreated like the tide,
Refusing to become his bride.
All this was to my hostess known,
For she my confidant had grown,

To whom the secrets of my breast,
As to a mother, were confess'd,
Who held that we must all be blind
To little faults if men were kind.
The chief objection in her view
(Though often urged and nothing new)
Was the disparity of years,
About which she express'd her fears,
Strongly advising me to pause
On character, and watch its flaws.

Bel. The wise decrees of nature's plan
Link'd woman's fate to that of man ;
Mutual companionship they own
Is better than to live alone.
By instinct both the sexes pair,
Betroth'd and bound like birds of air.
For this coy maidens sigh at home,
Or o'er the sea the wide world roam :
Warm-hearted, cheerful, and sincere,
Domestic life is woman's sphere ;
The crowning object of her life
Is centred in the name of wife ;
And if with offspring she is blest,
That bliss eclipses all the rest.

Mum. Incessantly had Zenos plied
On circuit, or when by my side,
Till to his suit I felt inclined
In Hymen's chains myself to bind,
And yield my hand if not my heart,
And so become his counterpart.
Thus fickle-minded ladies do,
When having some one else in view,
With their reluctant yes or no,
As if their minds they did not know,
In hope that those they love the best
Might reappear to make them blest.
No fairy palace in the skies
Except in vision, met my eyes,
No tidings, letter, or report,
Arrived my longing to support ;
Till as the tendril of the vine,
Or passion-flower, or sweet woodbine,
Dependent to the wall will cling,
I wedded with return of Spring.
    The interesting hour drew near,
In my new character to appear.
Around the altar's sacred fane,
Assembled were a numerous train

Of friends to see the holy rite,
By priests in orders who unite.
The marriage ceremony o'er,
Sweet flowers were scatter'd at the door,
By pretty nymphs all dress'd in white,
And maidens happy faced and bright,
Who in procession led the way,
Chanting in parts their roundelay,
Cheering the bridegroom and the bride,
To the state couch in liveried pride,
With favours and bouquets beside.

To the grand banquet all repair,
Th' *élite* and fairest of the fair,
In elegant costume of dress,
With all their charms of loveliness;
Where viands of the choicest kinds,
Delicious fruits and generous wines,
With rare exotic flowers' perfume,
And dazzling mirrors round the room;
Where taste and symmetry unite
To lure and fascinate the sight.
Good cheer elated old and young,
The hall with mirth and laughter rung,
And eloquence inspired the tongue.

The 'bride and bridegroom' toast went round,
And thrice the echoing walls resound,
With loud hurrahs and deaf'ning cheers,
When the bride blushing disappears.

   We made the usual monthly tour
On Nile's traditionary shore,
This sight to see, and there to stray,
To pass the honeymoon away,
In new Elysian fields to rove,
The haunts of love and silvan grove :
Then left the country for the town,—
The sunny smile for dingy frown,
The balmy air and tranquil skies,
For crowded streets and noisy cries ;
Where pleasure, fashion, pomp and pride,
With wealth and luxury reside.

Bel.   Did Mæris to your note reply,
Or file a bill in chancery?
Or did your husband, Mæris sue
At law for balance due to you ?

Mum.   He answered not, but kept aloof
From Zenos like a skulking wolf,
Who lurks in secret out of sight,
But covert breaks at dead of night.

His villainy so long conceal'd
Was soon in public court reveal'd,
And his deep guilt, obscured in haze,
Burst like a meteor into blaze.
Investigation left no doubt
Embezzlement had been found out.
To the indictable offence
The prisoner offer'd no defence :
Legions of witnesses on oath
(And I amongst the rest, though loth)
Swore Mœris had in his own name,
The rents received, and for the same
Given stamp'd receipts in his known hand,
For twenty years for farms and land.
All this was spent and fool'd away
In waste, extravagance, and play.
To mortgages he had confest,
With debts which led to his arrest.

The charge was tried,—the case was clear,
Ashamed he trembling shook with fear,
And when our eyes in flashes met,
Fring'd round with lashes black as jet,
And faces of Egyptian brown,
Made darker by th' expressive frown,

With th' ensemble, general style,
And vocal voice and beaming smile,
A family likeness you could trace
Of noble air and high-born race.
The judge from his exalted throne
In feeling words and solemn tone,
The criminal offence denounced,
And sentence of the court pronounced,—
"That being tried and guilty found,
On evidence so clear and sound,
Be exiled to a foreign clime,
For this felonious monstrous crime,
And punished as a felon there,
With labour, prison-dress, and fare."

Burck. 'Tis to be hoped more genial skies,
With future prospects did arise!—
Henceforward to enjoy, though late,
When settled down on your estate,
That paradise of bliss and love,
Angelic beings share above,
With Zenos, whose sagacious mind
Would out of chaos order find,
Some portion of the wreck to save
From jobber, Jew, and usurious knave.

Mum.   Life's pictured dreams of happiness
Resemble April's fickleness,
Whose brilliant rays illume the eye,
Till weather breeders flit the sky,
The presage to an augury ;
When gathering clouds begin to lour,
With thunder, lightning, tempest, shower.
Diminished to a speck in size,
The spoil became the wrecker's prize.
This tried the temper of my lord,
We no more pull'd with one accord,
Which led to bickering and dispute,
With wedlock's sour and bitter fruit.
A new discovery came to light,
Which threw all others out of sight :
Trembling I started,—look'd aghast
In wild despair upon the past,
Which gave to me a shuddering chill :
The wretch had forged my father's will !
Which stunned and paralyzed my tongue
In mute suspense, and midway hung.
As under some mysterious spell,
I gazed bewilder'd, swoon'd and fell.
While Zenos 'fore he read it half,
Burst into a hyena laugh.

I glanced him an indignant frown,
For he was cold and brutal grown,
And sneering growl'd 'your fortune's gone.'
   A will was proved, and contents sworn,
A few moons after I was born,
Which named him sole trustee and heir
(After providing for my care)
To all the property in charge,
Estates, lands, and investments large;
As if my sire his child forgot,
And she had never been begot.
The signature, though copied fair,
With Misraim's hand would not compare.
This glaring crime appeared too late,
And saved the culprit from his fate,
Else he'd indicted been and tried,
And by Egyptian law had died,
A malefactor hung in chains,
Without a grave for his remains.

Bel.   Here is the clue to what before
Was an enigma, and closed door,
When you by treachery were confin'd,
And sworn on oath insane of mind;
' In an asylum were immured,

And ne'er intended to be cured;'
But of the Will are you assured?

Mum. There lived an old domestic nurse,
Whom Mæris once was heard to curse,
Who whisper'd strange things in the ear,
Struck dumb and terrified with fear:
She on the night,—that fatal night,
My sire expired, discern'd a light,
And listening heard a footfall tread
(The slaves had all retired to bed)
In the still solemn midnight hour,
And heard the opening of a door,
Where my poor father breathed his last;
Turn'd pale with fright and look'd aghast
From the adjoining chamber, where
She heard strange footsteps loitering there;
Rummaging out an old scrutoire,
In my dear mother's pet boudoir;
Suspicious, nurse felt half inclined
To enter from a door behind,
And satisfy her curious mind.
Just as the watch-tower bell struck one,
And through the town its echoes run;
Some one emerged from the dark room,
Where all was silent as the tomb,

'And lightly trod the cracking floor.
And softly shut the creaking door,
From a wide crevice she look'd through,
She of some figure caught a view,
As it retreated with a light,
And vanish'd like a ghost of night;
She felt assured 'twas Mæris' shade,
And nervous shook, and felt afraid,
For he was at my father's side,
And o'er him watch'd until he died.
This faithful creature long had been
A favourite in the house, I ween,
Who in the service old had grown,
And like a heir-loom handed down
From my dear mother's family,
Of ancient blood and quality.
Mysteriously she disappear'd,
And suddenly, 'twas said and fear'd :
Some surmised poison,—some the knife,
But all believed she lost her life
By some foul crime ;—some crafty foe
In ambush struck the fatal blow !

Bel.   But could it be as you described,
That one so near of kin allied,

F

E'en under strong temptation, dare
To enter like a demon there ?
In the still hour of darkling night,
Where hazy peer'd the taper's light,
When the domestics were asleep,
And angels their lone vigils keep,
Prompted by evil spirits, break
The laws of God for lucre's sake,—
Clandestinely the titles steal,
And break the last will's mourning seal ?
In the dark chamber of the dead,
Whose spirit had so lately fled,
Whose pulse still beat,—whose flesh was warm,
And count'nance settling into calm,
Ere rigid grew those limbs in death,
And scarce had ceased th' expiring breath ?
While mute and senseless there he lay,
With open jaws, and eyes sky-grey,
With dew of death upon his cheek,
And looking as about to speak ;
When this old man of iron mould,
Death's chamber enter'd icy cold.
Could I that monster's visage scan,
And emblem Satan in the man,

It would be at the gates of Hell,
Arm'd with his cabalistic spell,
And prompting Mæris to the deed,
Which none of mortal mould conceived.
 Relentless doom and cruel fate
Your husband's love turn'd into hate ;
But then you link'd your fate and tied
The knot when you became his bride.
Mum. Alas ! a lot that thousands more
By one false marriage step deplore ;
Till grief, anxiety, and care,
Afflict and plunge us in despair.
Then I felt touched for womankind,
And sorrows of her brooding mind,
Secreted in her quivering breast,
When those she should have loved the best,
Her peace and happiness destroy,
And finds the gold mixed with alloy.
 Zenos display'd less love for me,
Than gold, or land, or harlotry,
And to his home inconstant grew,
And to his circuit practice flew
Without caress or fond adieu.
I always thought affection led
To confidence in those you wed ;—

That treasured secrets of the heart
Each to the other did impart,
As to a man of larger mind,
I like a satellite inclined,
Inquiringly look'd in his eyes,
To read their language and replies,
All that he coveted was gone,
Gambled and squandered, or in pawn,
Which soured his temper (none the best),
And his attachment put to test.

   Through this unsettled haze of night,
A glorious halo burst in sight,
Which all my dormant love revived,
For he I first loved still survived.
Italian skies and classic Rome
Attracted from his native home,
Where ancient custom still demands
That students travel foreign lands.
Illumin'd with a spiritual glow,
I felt my passion overflow,
As if enchantment round me hung,
And his dear image to me clung,
Forgetting that he came too late,
As I, alas! had seal'd my fate.

Burck.   The sexes, unto marriage given,
  Fulfil the laws of earth and heaven,—
  For social happiness combine,
  As well as to prolong their line
  Of ancestry, and imitate
  Dame Nature in her seedling state.
  Convenience, interest, or love,
  Will their united fitness prove,
  And often to their cost condemn
  The motives and designs of men,
  Or wily women who entice
  Their beaux to share their paradise.
Mum.   This idyll, at your wish begun,
  Nigh to its terminus has run ;
  Its incidents the past recall,
  Fill'd with the bitterness of gall,
  In narrative attire they seem
  The fictions of a shadowy dream ;
  Presented to the picturing mind
  In etchings of a mystic kind.
  Born under some malignant star,
  The world and I waged constant war ;
  From infancy to womanhood,
  On wave-bound rocks alone I stood

'Twixt heaven and earth in solitude:
And when the magic charm I tried,
And Zenos took me for his bride,
My evil genius follow'd still,
And plagued with every mortal ill.
Oh! say not life is but a span,
And at its close seems just began;
To me it was a journey long
And tedious, though cut off so young!
And now I shall unfold to view
My last dramatic scenes to you,
Whose virtuous principles impart
A moral lesson to the heart;—
Whose teaching, judgment, and advice,
Would purge from guilt, and wean from vice.

Burck.   Your narrative reveals a plot,
Which memory would wish to blot.

Mum.   Sethosis, who had just return'd,
Without the city walls sojourn'd.
Three Springs had wing'd their arrow flight,
Since he had vanished from my sight:
True as the dial to the sun,
My heart on him was fix'd upon;
I felt a warmer passion glow,
And through my vital system flow.

His princely form and noble air
Took captive many a maiden fair;
Bright and intelligent of face,
In all his actions, ease and grace.
I pined that he return'd too late,
And blamed myself I did not wait,
I heard he sympathised with me,
And shew'd regardful tendency;
Half disappointed I had wed,
He wish'd ' the poor old miser' dead.
Once in a low desponding key,
He cursed my uncle's villany;
And now neglected and ill used,
And of incontinence accused,
In soft regrets and broken sighs,
To me poured out his sympathies.
He taught me Zenos to despise;
I felt my indignation rise
As he his character pourtray'd,
And with ambiguous meaning said;—
' The future's useless to divine,
For being his, you can't be mine.'
These fatal words I ponder'd o'er,
Their dubious meaning to explore,

Like hovering fiends of hell in sight
They haunted me by day and night,
Now flattering with insidious art,
Which spread its venom through my heart;
Now tempting to commit a crime,
By plotting death before its time. .
Impell'd to action by despair,
I fell into the treacherous snare,
Against my husband to conspire,
To gratify a base desire.
Oh! that some arm had struck me dead,
Ere I conceived within this head,
So vile, so treacherous a design,
Or that the sun had ceased to shine
On deed of darkness such as mine,
So devilish black:—but now draw near,
That I may whisper in your ear,
For even now I shuddering fear;
As if his spirit hover'd nigh,
With weird-like furies rushing by.

Zenos was sick and kept his bed,
And as a wife I nursed and fed,—
Attended him with anxious care,
And kindly did his meals prepare

With my own hand, and solace gave,
In lieu of our old sable slave ;
And in his dietry one day,
As on the couch he sleeping lay,
Urged by some demon and inspired,
And, by a selfish motive fired,
Infused a poison in his cup,
And then,—and there,—I roused him up ;
Then handed with misgiving look
The season'd beverage which he took.
He lounged against the curtain'd wall,
Enveloped in his Indian shawl,
And soundly slept,—then gave a moan,
Which follow'd was by twitch and groan ;
He turn'd him round, and woke with pain,
But drowsy did not much complain,
And convalescent grew again.
    A guilty knowledge me appall'd,
And disappointment crush'd and gall'd,
The victim of malignant hate,
An orphan, and the sport of Fate !
' That dose,' cried some infernal power,
' If doubled would kill in an hour.'
I paused awhile on being foiled,
And conscience at the deed recoiled.

Once in the labyrinth of vice,
You follow where the imps entice,
Who deeper lead you into sin.
Again I dropt the poison in,
A double dose at breakfast time,
Best suited for such monstrous crime.
Without suspicion he withdrew,
With his accustomed cold adieu!
Perhaps ne'er to return alive
From Memphis' city's busy hive!
He parted in a sullen tune,
And prostrate was brought home at noon,
Suffering from colic,—sick with pain,
And wind that blew a hurricane.
The doctor came,—his nostrums tried,
And pour'd emetics in a tide;
With opiates lull'd him into sleep,
Which caused me to relent and weep.
Exhausted, senseless, there he lay,
And waked not till return of day,
But nothing said; he loath'd his food,
And sunk into a drowsy mood.
The doctor, standing by his bed,
His slow pulse felt and shook his head;

The eyes were fix'd, and rigid grew,
And from his face the colour flew,
While the breath gently ebb'd away,
And there unconsciously he lay ;
Death's rattles told that all was o'er,
And he had fled this earthly shore.

Burck.   Conspiring, rebel angels fell
From highest heaven to lowest hell :
The tact and craft of womankind
Are far more subtle than mankind.
By hatching plots you damn'd your soul
To misery at that awful goal,
Where phantoms of the living type
Exist in spiritual stereotype ;
Transparent forms of human mould,
Ethereal essences and cold,
Where they repine for sins of earth,
And curse the authors of their birth ;
Fill'd with anxiety and care,
They rave in agonised despair.

'Tis thought these torments purify,
And fit for Paradise on high,
Proportion'd to the life we spend,
And not eternal without end,
As priests or prophet bards pretend.

God is all merciful and just,
And knew our frailties from the first.
Amenable to human law,
The convict standing at the bar
Of justice is condemn'd to die,
Or exiled into slavery !
And when eternal life begins,
His soul still suffers for its sins.
But say not God's less just than man,
Or unforgiving in his plan,
Or that he is vindictive, bent
On everlasting punishment,
As if he were a monster grown,
And not the righteous God we own.

Mum.   Your episode has split in two
The narrative reveal'd to you :
List to the sequel, I'll be brief,
For minds o'ercharged require relief.
Since death I have unconscious lain,
And pray my corpse may here remain.
When living I was prone to think
There was a natural binding link
Between its casket and the soul ;
We traced the former to its goal :

But of that ignis fatuus spark
Of life that glitters in the dark,
The jewell'd soul, I nothing know,
Whether on earth or realms below.
If to it transmigration 's given,
We may unite again in heaven,
Not that I 've faith in such a leaven,
As the gross parts dissolve and rise
In floating atoms to the skies.

Let us again return to shore :
After the obsequies were o'er
Of Zenos, and the nervous shock,
I grew as hard as flint or rock,
And as a Polar iceberg cold,
So wither'd up was he and old !
In mourning costume I was clad,
Reserved and silent, though not sad,
Beheld a brighter prospect near
In one I loved and held so dear,
And hugg'd his image to my breast,
Expecting to be heavenly blest.

Sethosis called when I was out,
And paused ere entering as in doubt ;
Inquiry solved the rumoured tale,
And he absorb'd turned deadly pale,

And without card or word withdrew,
As if to avoid an interview.
After the showy funeral
I waited, but he did not call
Or write, or slightest notice take,
Though all I did was for his sake.
Bewildered I began to doubt,
And took the means to find it out;
But when I asked the reason why,
Sethosis sent a cold reply,
Which nettled, vexed, and mortified
My spirit, dignity, and pride.
He goaded me the act to do,
And then deserting me withdrew;
I taunted him with wishing dead
My husband, but he would not wed.

   Disconsolate, abandon'd, sad,
The voice of conscience drove me mad;
I scorn'd the wretch that could deceive,
And loath'd myself who could conceive
So vile a plot, so base a crime
As murdering one before his time,
When in frail health, and unprepared.
Oh! how his eyeballs rolled and stared

While in excruciating pain,
Nor did suspect nor aught complain.
His spectre haunted me at night,
I could not rid it from my sight;
Where'er I went it did pursue,
Accusing and upbraiding too ;
Till plung'd in fathomless despair,
And fill'd with bitterness and care,
Did I resolve by my own hand
To die by the same means I planned ;
But with a scornful woman's hate,
All furious to revenge her fate,
And curse th' adulterer who fled,
Who had defiled her marriage bed.
To this abhorrent carnal deed,
To my disgrace I guilty plead :—
' May all the plagues which Moses spread
Through Egypt, light upon his head;
May every mortal ill o'ertake,
And marrow-bone and fibre ache;
May every known disease attack,
And be as pungent as the rack ;
The air be tainted with his breath,
With settled blight and lingering death :

May he be struck deaf, dumb, and blind,
And throughout life deranged in mind;
Unquenchable his feverish thirst,
Tormented and by demons curst;
Be miserable unto life's end,
A wand'rer without home or friend!
May all he eats like ashes burn,
And all he drinks to poison turn:
Painful and sleepless the long night,
And nervous at all sounds take fright;
May horrors him deprive of sleep,
And hissing serpents round him creep;
Let scorpions bite,—mosquitos tease,
And suck his blood up to the lees.
May grisly spectres reappear,
And all his dreams be fill'd with fear,
May wintry age and slow decay,
Wither his faculties away;
And when life's scenes are acted through,
And falling curtain hides from view,
May he in cold oblivion rot
Without a grave, and be forgot;
His soul in purgatory dwell,
To suffer all the pangs of hell!"

Bel. The world's a drama and a show,

Where emigrants pass to and fro,—

A stage whereon each acts a part,

Ere they the busy scenes depart ;

Life active is a flowing stream,

Which to review appears a dream.

Mum. An outcast and without a friend,

I wish'd the world engulphed would end.

Forsaken, desolate, and sad,

My guilty conscience drove me mad,

No peace of mind was left to me,

But wretchedness and misery.

In meditation and in prayer,

For the great change did I prepare,

A suicide about to die,

And plunge into eternity !

Oh ! that the death-sleep all embrace,

Would end the sufferings of our race !

That we might cease to live again,

And in unconsciousness remain !—

That vital spark and heavenly guest,

The tenant of the brain or breast,

Dissolve to atoms of the air,

When disembodied, is my prayer !

G

My mortal crimes may God forgive,
But suffer not my soul to live!
   With one lamp's solitary gloom,
I sought retirement in my room,
Resign'd to meet my awful doom
In penitence, despair, and tears,
And fill'd with supernatural fears;
For apparitions flitted round,
And phantom forms sprang from the ground.
Absorbed, reflecting, and alone,
I drank the cup of poison down.
This was a solemn thinking hour,
When worlds around began to lour,
And I grew dizzy at each breath,
Awaiting the great teacher Death,
As standing on the brink of hell,
In a deep trance, or mystic spell;
While meditating on the soul,
Its nature, origin, and goal,
My vital parts felt agonised,
And intellects were paralyzed,
A stupor all my senses drown'd,
I giddy felt,—the room turn'd round,
And I sank lifeless on the ground.

To you, Sirs, and to you alone,
Are these dire revelations known ;
To none beside have I confess'd
These lock'd up secrets of my breast,
Which has discharged a load of grief,
And to my mind dispensed relief :
May sleep's oblivion hide my shame
For ever, and blot out my name,
As if I'd never been begot,
Or lost to memory, forgot !

CONCLUSION.

As we were crawling through the tombs
And alleys of these catacombs,
A flock of bats flapp'd out our light,
Which left us in the realms of night
And utter darkness, without guide
To lead our footsteps : side by side,
Groping upon our hands and knees,
As through a mine of galleries ;
Crushing the bones that lie about,
But could not find the exit out.
The dreary hours pass'd slowly by,
And no deliverance seem'd nigh ;

The mazy windings of the cave,
Threaten'd us with a living grave ;
And streets of tombs were traversed o'er,
Ere we could find the entrance door ;
When in the distance to the right,
We saw a needle's eye of light,
Attracting as it wider grew,
To the façade we entered through.

PICTORIAL SEA VIEWS.

PICTORIAL SEA VIEWS.

I.—(Night.)

Drawn like a curtain round our hemisphere,
The shadowy wings of Night descending spread:
Benumbing sleep imprisons half the world
In temporary oblivion: the haunts of men
Are silent as the chambers of the dead!
The crescent moon's on watch,—the starry sky,
With thousand solar systems like our own,
Unfolds infinity and endless space!
The boundless waves in rolling volumes rise
Rejoicing as they roam the azure fields,
Circuitous as belts around the waist
Of Jupiter; or tipp'd with silvery foam
As luminous as Saturn's golden rings.
While from yon rocky cliff above, amid
The agitated waters, I beheld
Through a long tube of magnifying power,

A panorama of the glassy deep ;
With stirring scenes and incidents of life
E'er on the change; and in this bird's-eye view
Of heaven's reflecting mirror, there arose
Successive views of those who plough the sea,
And circumnavigate the wondrous globe!

II.—(The Ocean.)

Dark rolling Ocean! unfathomable gulf!
Tumultuous as the restless thoughts of men,
Chartless thy mazy windings, and obscure
Thy origin and being,—use and end.
Like to a rushing cataract, the tide
Swells in thy bosom spreading far and wide,
Wasting its strength upon the shingly shore,
Kissing the fettering hills and chalky cliffs,
Till spent by its own fury it withdraws
Its mountain waves, and sinks into a calm
And placid slumber in its lulling bed,
As if subdued and fed with magic oil,
Which soothes and hushes in a soft embrace
The child-like passion of the angry flood.

Nought with thy vastness can compare on earth ;
The desert, mountain, prairie, plain or steppes

Sink into insignificance with thee,

In spacious grandeur and sublimity !

These bear the yoke of man's despotic rule,

At whose command, temples and cities rise,

And at his bidding fall ! but over thee

Proud mistress of the deep's inhabitants

Who was from the beginning, and is now

The masterpiece of all terrestial works

He has no power ! Thou spurn'dst him* in thy pride

Who came to gird thee with his bridge of boats.

Supreme of earth he was no match for thee !

Thou didst arise in awful majesty,

Which threatened to ingulf the trembling land,

And scatter'd to the wind his manacles :

All powerful and indignant at the pride,

And vain presumption of the martial host.

    Another† of imperial dignity

Sat on the shore and bade the rising tide

Stop at his feet, submissive, and retire !

But did it heed his arrogant command ?

Or with more force than idle words roll on

Rejoicing and submerging all the land,

Spurning the monarch with defiant roar ?

       * Xerxes.   † Canute.

III.—(INVASION.)

How many tales thy history could impart
From early infancy, ere arts arrived
To such perfection, as enabled man
To court acquaintance with Thee, roaming flood,
And join the ends of earth in wedlock's chain,
Holding communion with the piecemeal world,
When the canoe was hollow'd from the tree,
And the wild Indian learn'd to fish for food,
And scour the forest for the flying game.

Surrounded by the broad Atlantic flood,
These dwarfish dotted islands of the sea
Became the prey of Cæsar when he cross'd
From Europe's continent to Britain's cliffs,
Opposed by islanders who flew to arms,
And bravely met th' invader on the beach,
Fighting like lions for their fatherland;
As in our time the forest tribes dispute
Our friendly visits for commercial gain,
Or conquest of hereditary soil,
Or missionary labour to convert
From superstitious faith the Indian tribes
In New South Wales or the Pacific isles.

Tradition gives the glory and the praise
To the great Alfred our law-giving king,
Who first raised Britain to imperial place,
And arm'd her with a fleet of men-of-war ;
To combat with the vagrants* of the sea,
Who came in hostile force to spy the land,
And pillage, seize, and burn th' invaded coast.
The heptarchy divided, then unite
For self-defence against the common foe,
With galleys of superior size and strength,
To thwart the plundering corsair and defeat.
This school'd and form'd their naval character,
Born, bred, and cradled in their wooden walls,
Old England's safeguard and her element.

IV.—(THE FLOOD.)

The earth lies open to the search of man,
And he hath scann'd it curiously through
From pole to pole, the mountain and the mine.
The heavens above he visits and describes,
Examining the multitude of worlds,
Their distance and dimensions measuring ;
And classes into systems all the stars,

* Danes.

Giving infinity and space a map
To guide the young astronomer to heaven !
But the deep sea lies hidden from his search,
An undiscovered fathomless abyss.
Master of all, man cannot conquer this,
Though his ambition has united seas,
And into other channels rivers turn'd.

   Oh ! for a visit to the interior deep !
To view the ancient strata of the Earth
In its primeval and unfashioned form,
As it rose out of chaos all deform'd,
Shapeless and void, an undigested mass ;
While the fermenting waters foam'd around
In agitated murmurs to the shore,
As if disturb'd by some leviathan ;
When thunders shook the surges from the bed,
Which like a cavern yawn'd, and billows roll'd
In volumes o'er the raging element,
Forth burst th' imprisoned waters rushing down
From hill to vale, and rocks which scatter'd lay
In broken ridges on each other piled ;
Forming the wild cascade or cataract,
Which leap'd from rock to rock in silvery foam,
Hewing a passage to the sloping glen

Of chisel'd smoothness through the earthquake's rent,
Which drip of ages into chasms wore,
And split up the foundations of the world,
And tore in fragments, tossing to and fro
The solid quarries of a time remote,
Anterior to the mythic age of man !

V.—(DISCOVERIES.)

The light of genius first conceived the Earth
From its reflected shadow on the moon
In an eclipse, to be a circling sphere !
Americus adopted the idea
Of its rotundity, and sailing round
The fragments of a world in seas engulphed
(Romantic vision of a daring mind),
In ignorance commenced, without a chart,
To guide his wandering footsteps o'er the deep,
And found a world across th' Atlantic's flood.

Columbus follow'd, sanguine of a prize,
Exposed to toils and hardships of the sea,
And threatened violence of a hostile crew,
Till open mutiny in murmurs broke.
Through day and night he plough'd his watery way
O'er tracks unknown, and waves unrid before,

'Midst perils of the deep, where howling winds
Mix their hoarse voices with the angry storm,
And breaking surges with their white foam roll,
And waterspouts hang threat'ning in the air.
The anxious admiral, inspired with hope,
Buoys up the flagging spirits of his men
With promise of success and rich reward
From day to day : their spirits rise and fall,
Alternately amid such hopes and fears,
And ever and anon at break of day,
They look for land, and sigh to look in vain !
Until the helmsman ever on the watch,
Rivets his eye upon a misty speck,
Which gradually emerges into view,
' Land, land,' he cries, and steers toward the shore,
Fixing his eyes on solid earth once more !
  Magellan the Pacific first explored,
And threw a charm o'er modern enterprise,
Which kindred souls in rivalry outvied.
The fearless Cortes conquered Mexico,
And there display'd the chivalry of Spain.
Pizzaro found the riches of Peru,
And mines of wealth flowed into Europe's ports.
The enterprising Drake was on their track

In search of plunder, conquest, and revenge,
And galleons laden with the precious ore,
And in his voyage through the South Seas sail'd,
Discovering countries unknown before,
(Since grown familiar as our island home),
And to his honour and his country's pride
Completed the first voyage round the world!
The light of science then began to dawn,
And inspiration to emit its rays ;
Adventurous spirits into action launch'd,
To solve th' enigma and disperse all doubt.

VI.—(The Armada.)

Jealous of England's power and rivalry,
The haughty Spaniard, chivalrous and strong,
Sought to revenge him on our maiden Queen,
Who in her dignity rose to dispute
The conquest and dominion of the seas ;
Superior in numbers, weight and size,
The proud Armada, after long delay,
Appear'd exulting in defiant wrath
With his o'erwhelming fleet upon our shores ;
To annihilate our navy, and to scourge
And humble England for imagined wrongs.

Then did th' heroic Queen assume command
At Tilbury, and in the midst appear
Surrounded by her generals of renown ;
And through the elated ranks rode out on horse,
To cheer, inspire, and fill with flattering hope
The hearts which march to conquest or to death !
   An evil omen in the sky gave sign ;
The elements themselves began the war
With roaring whirlwind and the tempest storms,
Which proved our ablest and our best allies,   .
And scatter'd to the winds their naval force ;
And headlong drove the giant and the dwarf
In violent collision and rebound :
The shatter'd sails were rent,—the masts were split
And broken up in fragments like a reed
Amid the breakers which devoured the spoil :
Some waterlogged sunk in the deep sea's trough
And left a swell which drew in others near,
While many drifting to the rocky shore,
To pieces fell and perish'd with their crews.
The storm subsided, and the English fleet
Then hove in sight to give the final blow,
And fell with desperate fury on the foe,
Who offered slight resistance, and became

A shattered remnant of a powerful fleet,
The sport and the derision of the world.

VII.—(NAVIGATORS.)

The globe has been developed year by year
With each succeeding voyage, and the whole,
Isles, continents and seas group'd in a chart,
And christened as discovered with a name
Immortal ! registered in rolls of fame !
Raleigh and Anson, with Perouse and Cook,
Ross, Parry, Franklin, and inferior stars,
Rank in the firmament of Earth's renown ;
Who introduced and knit in harmony
The scatter'd tribes and nations of this globe,
Drawing the many distant countries near
In bonds of friendship, merchandise and trade.
　Ten thousand fleets sweep o'er thy liquid plain,
The great highway of nations round our sphere,
The element of freedom on whose breast
The navies of all countries ride at large,
And through whose briny flood from east to west,
From north to south, where navigable seas,
And distant inland rivers them invite ;

With canvass spread they sail from clime to clime,
Collecting the wreck'd treasures of the deep.

VIII.—(THE EQUATOR.)

The progress of the New World hastens on;
Man is advancing, still much more remains
To be discover'd of the split-up Earth,
Whose limbs united form one glorious whole
On a revolving globe, upon whose disc
Each country's mark'd and lined into degrees,
With the great belts of water spread around
The barren mountains of a half drown'd world,
Through which the navigation of the sea
Has thread its way, and vast discoveries made
On either side th' equator which divides
And separates the old world from the new,
Midway between th' extremes of either pole.

Oh! what a world would this appear to one
Launch'd into life upon the briny flood
Of a tumultuous all-surrounding sea!
If bred on it from his first peep of day
Up to the glimmering dawn of reasoning years;
Without his having once refresh'd his sight
With the all fruitful earth; or aught has seen

But the green waters rolling at his feet,
And the blue vault of Heaven above his head.

IX.—(FISHERMEN.)

The curtain rises and unfolds to view
Some glimpses of the ever changing scene
Passing before us in this voyage of life.
Unseen within its billowy bosom roam
The finny race and monsters of the deep;
Who in their native element disport,
Joyous and happy, their short span of life,
And prey upon each other for their food.
Heaven in its mercy e'er provides for man,
And myriads of fish supply his wants.
The patient fishermen, with hidden snares,
Together muster in their little smacks,
And ply their trade through midnight's dreary hours.
In absence of the sun's refulgent light :
Returning to the land at early dawn,
With freighted nets of various kinds of spoil,
To reap the harvest of their midnight toil.

X.—(SAILOR.)

The son of Neptune, cradled in his bark,
Dreams not of danger while he tempts the main.

But blithely singing sails securely o'er
Thy mountain waves and fathomless abyss,
Though treacherous rocks his vessel undermine,
Or monsters lurk expectant of their prey.
How much of suffering's silently endured,
By him who left the old paternal roof,—
Domestic quiet and the fondest hearts,
To brave the hardships of seafaring life !
Coop'd in his narrow craft from month to month,
And promenading to and fro the deck.
The dull monotony of sea and sky
Is ever present : if a distant sail
Diminish'd to a speck appears in view,
'Tis watch'd with interest till it fades from sight ;
His weather-beaten face and sun tann'd hide,
Stamp him of Nature's rough and iron mould,
Accustom'd to the hardships of a life
Of toil and peril in the treacherous deep.
Full to the brim of kindness, love and joy,
Of manners bluff, and independent ease,
With much of open character to please,
There beats beneath a heart of tenderness.
A friend to discipline and quiet rule,
He takes his turn to watch upon the bridge,

Or at the wheel in solemn midnight hour,
Giving the signal to his steering mate,
With eye on compass, and the distant sail,
To guide the vessel on her devious course,
From dangerous contact or the coral reef.

XI.—(STEAMER.)

Like specks upon the ocean, vessels glide
On sails of canvass swelling to the wind,
Which carries them majestically through
The foaming billows, guided in their track
By him who at the rudder steers ahead :
Sailing along they make for diff'rent ports
By chart and compass, steadily and slow.
Dim in the distance swiftly flies along,
As if pursuing, and out sailing fast,
Behold a modern rover of the sea
Puffing up wreaths of smoke across the skies,
Which issues from a funnel in mid air.
Her speed annihilates both time and space,
Impell'd by steam she carries all before,
Bridging the gulf that separates each shore,
Intwining nations in a fond embrace
Of friendship, trade, and interchange of thought.

XII.—(Smuggler.)

Yonder's the lawless smuggler's desperate crew,
With courage arm'd and instruments of death,
Silently stealing through the shades of night;
Who with keen watchfulness approach the shore
Suspicious of discovery. The wary band
Slack sail and pause, and search with telescope
The neighbouring coast, and listen as in doubt,
Ere they prepare to run the boat aground,
Beneath a beetling cliff or shelter'd cove,
To land their contraband, and quick depart.
Mute and confounded they behold a fire
Upon the distant hill, which beacon warns
Like telegraph the bold adventurous crew,
Who tack about, and in th' obscuring mist
Of night envelop'd, watching still the shore,
Blustering with disappointment make escape;
Cursing with angry oaths the coastguard watch,
Who follows with his glass the smuggling sail.

XIII.—(Volcano.)

Light shines above the ridge of clouds on high,
And sparks of fire illume the darken'd sky,

Breaking the seal of night and still repose ;
For yonder pyramidal mountain frowns,
'Mid a dense atmosphere of curling smoke,
And from its centre shakes the solid earth
With stifled groans of agony within
Its hollow chambers ; rumbling with a noise
Which, hissing through the deep volcano's throat,
Like an explosion of artillery bursts,
Rattling in peals of thunder through the air,
And round the trembling hills in echo dies.
A blaze of fire illumes the scenery near,
While boiling streams of lava pouring down
Like liquid furnaces the mountain's sides,
Threat'ning destruction in its wayward course !
The sea is like a glittering mirror lit,
And boats with living freights put out from shores
To view the grand eruption ; while on land
In shelter'd places human figures swarm,
To animate the landscape far and near.
Alternately the smoke and flames ascend,
And scoria and stones descend in showers,
While fate seems pointing to a horrid doom,
And nature at the ruin looks aghast !

XIV.—(OVERBOARD.)

The earth revolves and slowly shadows forth
Another picture rising from the sea,
Expanding and developing its lines,
Like a dissolving view, and disappears.

The mariner from whaling homeward turns,
After long absence, to his native shores,
Cheered with the hope of meeting long-lost friends,
And the fair maid engaged to be his bride;
When danger unforeseen his prospects thwarts.
O'er the ship's side as nimbly he sprung
On to the gunwale's narrow slippery ledge
Some tackle to adjust he missed his hold,
And backward fell into the opening gulf,
With a loud splash which raised a louder shout
Of "a man overboard!" from head to stern,
When every tar spontaneous flies to help.
The buoy is overthrown that he may float,—
The sails are furled to stop the vessel's flight,—
The claw-like anchor cast,—the helm is turn'd,
The boat is lower'd, manned with a gallant crew,
Who quickly row towards the reckon'd spot;
With watchful eye they search the mazy flood

And call aloud, but answer none receive :
Then rest upon their sculls and list to hear.
The rude wind mocks their silence, while the roar
Of splashing billows drowns the stifled voice.
Again they ply their oars and think they hear
His faint voice breaking through the murmuring breeze,
And search the broad expanse of sea around
For a full hour.   Alas! the closing waves
Had overwhelm'd him in a wat'ry grave.
Keen disappointment saddens every face,
And a warm tear is dash'd from every eye,
As with full hearts like mourners they return
To the ship's side without their missing mate.

XV.—(A WRECK.)

The panoramic change again reveals
Another etching of the dangerous deep.
Oh ! how the feelings in the bosom yearn,
When the astonish'd sight beholds afar
The floating fragments of a scatter'd wreck !
How will the silent speaking countenance
Express the mind's emotion, and grow pale
As if a blight had settled on the cheek,
Its freshness withering ! there piece by piece

With drifting cargo scatter'd all around,
Look like the ruins of a noble bark,
Which haply sailing to her destined port,
Driven by the wind upon some sunken rock
With violence struck! then like a cradle
On her beam ends rocks, struggling for freedom;
Her pumps unequal to the rising flood,
And dropsical beyond the cure of art:
Her parting timbers warn the hardy crew,
Who taking to the long-boat roam the seas,
And are the sport of every rolling wave;
Engulph'd and disappearing in the whirl
Of angry waters dashing them with spray.
Deep in the north the polar star is set,
On which their eager eyes are fix'd in hope!
The sun and moon alternately appear
Without a sail or speck of land to cheer
Their drooping spirits: spent with constant toil,
Hunger and thirst, with burning heat, assail,
And goad them on like cannibals half mad,
To the last dreadful act of casting lots!

XVI.—(PIRATE.)

Another background scene appears in view!
The vagrant pirate's home is on the sea,

Where night and day he plies his horrid trade;
Lurking like cunning tiger in his lair,
To spring upon his unsuspecting kind,
Out from some hidden creek or river's mouth,
Where with his glass he watches for his prey.
Swift as a meteor through the sky he darts
With all his canvas spread. The distant sail
Too late discovers them upon her track,
And with all speed flies from the outlawed band,
But flies in vain; the corsair's bark gains on
The sluggish trader with a broadside fire:
The merchant captain yields not, nor his crew,
Without a struggle: they the anchor drop,
Sails furl, and lying down on deck receive
The heavy broadside of the privateer,
Whose thunders rattle and whose lightnings glare.
The vessels lie alongside and are lash'd,
And man to man in murderous fray is set.
The battle rages and the combatants
Wax fierce and warm, and thin each others ranks;
The clashing steel and instruments of death
Work dreadful slaughter, and the groans of men
In agony mix in the din of strife.
The daring outlaw overpowers his foe,

(Reduced in number) and the vessel boards :
Mowing like grass the brave defending crew,
Who still contend and every inch dispute,
With superhuman strength and mad despair.
The mate's heroic courage and the skill
With which he deals his blows inspire his men,
Who give no quarter to the knife-arm'd band.
At last the remnant fly like badgers dogg'd,
Followed by monsters thirsting for their blood,
T" escape whose wrath they leap into the flood.

XVII.—(COLLISION.)

The murderous strife dissolves as on we gaze
Like shadowy fancies of a future world,
And is succeeded by another piece
On the dramatic stage of ocean life ;
When night has spread her mantle o'er the deep,
And slumber seals the eyelids of the crew ;
The shock of a collision vibrates through,
That shakes the vessel to her very keel
As if a treacherous rock beneath them lay,
And tore up all her timbers with a crash !
Stunn'd, nude, and flying, the affrighted crew
Trembling like ghosts roused from the nether shades,

Confused and breathless to the deck up flew,
To learn the fatal news.   The sinking ship
Reels paralysed and to and fro she rocks.
A heavy mist encompass'd all around,
And through the canvas shrieked the wind aloud,
Mocking some wailing voices ! on she rolls
To their amazement, and the fearful truth
Which flash'd across the mind is now reveal'd.
The earthquake shock that fill'd them with alarm,
Was of two traders meeting in a fog,
And viewless to each other ! thunder clouds
Met in the stormy sky are not more fierce,
When the electric fluid them explodes,
And every hill reverberates the roar ;
Or the collision of a railway train
Meeting another on the fatal line,
Rebounds and crushes to an utter wreck.
Like a great whale the schooner roll'd and turned,
O'erwhelmed she rose as in convulsive throbs,
And lurching disappeared with all on board !
Alas ! their frantic cries and wild despair,
Sound like the viewless spirits of the deep.

XVIII.—(Ship on Fire.)

From this sad spectacle of night we turn
To the horizon with its blaze of light.
Enveloped in a cloud, a sheet of flame,
As of a fiery mountain, spouting out
Of its wide nostrils liquid streams of fire!
Which roll in torrents down its heaving breast,
Encompass'd with thick columns of black smoke,
Illuminating sea, and earth, and sky,
Ascending and descending rain of fire!
So through the curling mist appears the blaze,
Feeding upon the entrails of a ship!
Alas! the frantic inmates cannot fly
The floating castle of the briny flood;
But scorched by the devouring element,
Run wild with pain about the fiery deck,
And in despair plunge headlong in the sea!
Some cut away the tackle of the boat,
Which dangling hung over the vessel's side,
Hoping to save a remnant of the crew;
But in their eagerness the boat upset.
The pumps were work'd and every effort made,
But stifling smoke and flame enveloped all!

XIX.—(POLAR REGIONS.)

From this exciting scene we further look
To scenes remote and desolate as death,
Where winter's solitary torpid face
Gives out no sign of life;—where sluggish night
Reposes calmly half the sunless year,
Draped in her fleecy whiteness, mid the blocks
Of frozen water, and perpetual snow!
Beneath the pole-star in the cold sky set,
These realms in solitary grandeur look
Inanimate and dead without a sun
To cheer their pale complexion, overgrown
With frozen icebergs and eternal snows,
The livery of winter! Beneath the mass
Which ages have been rearing on its back,
Rolling in darkness,—struggling in its tomb
The ocean lies, and like an earthquake heaves,
The iceberg fields, which with the billows rise
Like mountain chains which midway cross the sky.
There hoarse groans rend their adamantine ribs,
Muttering their sullen thunder through the air.
    In these inclement climes and dreary wastes,
Which bring no interchange of night and day,

But where perpetual darkness reigns around,
The frozen whale ships bedded in the ice,
Look like deserted castles of the air ;
The fabulous creations of romance,
And still as death without a sign of life.
Yet they have tenants who excursions make
To pass the tedious winter months away,
Till the return of Spring breaks the huge blocks,
And opens up a passage to the sea,
That they may ply their dull and patient trade,
And freight their vessels with the generous oil.

In these wild regions perish'd Franklin's men,
Shut up in thick ribb'd ice from year to year,
And thither track'd by Clintock, who at last
The problem solved of their disastrous fate,
And found some relics of the missing crew,
With the commander's solitary grave !

In these eternal solitudes exist
The dreary life which commonly abounds
In the remotest corners of the world ;
The vegetable kingdom quite shut out,
Fruits, flowers and edibles scarce ever seen.
Blank, dormant, lifeless all around appears
And so has lain for ages ; human life

Is scant, and miserable Esquimaux
And Innuits look the remnant of a race
Worn out, abandon'd to a lingering death.
Wild animals that over-run the earth,
And dwell in dreary wilds remote from man,
Are limited; arctic bears and seals,
With a stray deer, or hare, or hardy bird,
And the leviathans that swim the flood,
Give signs of life and motion at the Pole,
O'er which the funeral pall of death is hung.

XX.—(EMIGRANT.)

Another scene presents itself to view,
As the dissolving one at last withdrew.
Some for their health are sent across the sea,
And daily rough the horrors of a voyage,
For more congenial climes and brighter skies,
In order to prolong declining life.
While some explore the hidden parts of earth,
In opposite extremes of heat and cold,
Through distant seas to lands untrod before,
And search with zeal each new discover'd shore,
For purposes of science, conquest, trade!
But many more forsake their fatherland,

I

O'ergrown with numbers like a hive of bees,
From disappointment, poverty, and crime,
And seek an Eden in the promised land,
Founding a colony in wilds remote.

Attracted from the old world to the new,
The emigrant, with all he owns most dear,
Embarks on board the ark that swarms with life,
And braves the dangers of the teeming deep,
Whose surges toss him midway to the sky,
And then as suddenly leap down th' abyss,
Plunging and swallowing in a rude embrace
The struggling bark, the sport of wind and wave.
Mute, sick and solitary, he's cast down,
Holding communion with his stifled thoughts;
And while the flying ship pursues its way
To the antipodes, Janus-like he turns
To take a last, fond, lingering farewell,
Of that dear isle fast fading from his sight;
O'er which he muses sorrowful and sad !

XXI.—(Transportation.)

Another illustration now behold,—
A limb diseased is severed from the tree !
Behold, the transport getting under weigh,

Freighted with felons manacled in chains !
Confin'd below, the freedom of the deck
Is granted as a favour, not a right,
O'erwatch'd and guarded by the armed marines.
Crime has its penalties across the main,
In some remote outlandish colony,
The dread abode of rude and savage life,
Where, toiling in his fetters like a slave ;
The convict lives without a ray of hope
To cheer him in his penal servitude.

    With peals of laughter mixed with boisterous mirth
And sprightly levity, they meet their doom
Of banishment, insensible to shame ;
Wilful, corrupt, and vicious in their lives,
The very scum of loose society,
And victims of their own degenerate crimes.
Humiliated in a convict's dress,
With shaven head and prison discipline,
Their mothers scarce would know them in disguise !
But there is one alas ! who keeps aloof,
Mute, sorrowful and lonely in the throng :
Superior in birth, attainments, caste,
And education which exalts the soul,
Filling it with nobility of thought :

He has no fellowship with vulgar minds,
But feels abash'd in such low company ;
Struggling with conscience he is seen to weep,
And dwelling on the past, upbraids, deplores
His lost position, and the forgery
Which has consigned him to a felon's doom,
And all the bitter pangs of deep remorse.

XXII.—(WAR.)

Would that the world were knit in bonds of peace,
And war with its calamities unknown,
That man might realize a heaven below,
In lieu of drawing on the future one
His fancy conjures up, with hope deferr'd ;
But his ambition, avarice, desire,
Let loose and uncontroll'd, to conquest lead,
And with it half the miseries of life !

Lo! on th' horizon resting like a cloud,
A fleet of war ships now give eager chase,
And rove the ocean wide in hot pursuit
Of fugitives with whom they are at war,
Whose ships escaped through favour of the night.
List to the echo of the cannon's roar,
Which flies along the surface of the deep,

And calls the hostile flag to deadly feud !
Who, brave and strong, their enemy defy,
And through the cannon's throat send their reply;—
Accept the challenge, anchor drop, sails furl,
And for the coming conflict all prepare
To fight and conquer, or like heroes die.
   Oh ! what a message in that broadside peal,
That flash of lightning, and that thunder's roar!
As every ship approached and station took
Alongside those they were in combat join'd.
The grappling irons to the masts were lash'd,
And face to face and hand to hand they met.
Their steel flash'd fire amidst the deadly strife,
Their rifles crack'd,—explosions shook the air,
The blasted lungs of cannon roar'd aloud,
And clouds of smoke obscured the hostile scene.
Through various success, 'mid hope and fear,
The battle rages and is at its height,
And the fierce contest lays its victims low.
On either side the dying and the slain,
Together heap'd, formed ramparts for the fight ;
Their ranks mowed down, and thinn'd upon the deck,
Invite the foe to board the crippled ship,
With pike in hand, in closer combat join'd,
Till every man's cut down, or pris'ner yields.

A loud explosion burst upon the ear,
A ship on fire illuminates the Heavens,
And frightful cries fill all with wild despair.
Danger impels to flight, and some escape,
While some run foul, and soon are prizes made.
Diversion spreads confusion through the line
And shifts the scene of battle, but the fight
Renew'd with double fury still prevails,
And slaughter thins the ranks of either side ;
Till, half their ships disabled, they retire
Exhausted, yet inspired to daring deeds,
For honour, country, friends, by all held dear ;
Till fortune gives the battle to the strong,
And scatters to the wind a noble fleet,
With pride and power, and pageantry of war.
　　Oh ! what a wreck and ruin of the past
Present themselves at morning's early dawn,
When all is calm and still ! a funeral scene,
With the death groans of wounded bleeding men.
As the eye ranges o'er the battle field,
And feeds upon the grim and spectral waste
Of human carnage,—mastless, shrouded ships,
The floating fragments of the scatter'd wreck,
The hulks and bodies thrown upon the shore,

The sufferings of the maim'd, the wealth consumed,
And all the sad realities of war!

XXIII.—(SLAVERY.)

The battle wanes from sight and fades away !
Transferring us to Afric's fever'd coast
Teeming with life ; its sons of sable hue,
Inferior in creation and in soul,
Poor, outcast, animal, debased,
In slavery are consign'd to foreign shores,
Without distinction as to sex or age !
The negro race is merchandise for sale,
And sold like cattle in the neighbouring fair,
Or market-place for gold—which all enslaves ;
Before which men in every grade of life
Become idolators and bow the knee
With a devotion fitter for a god !
Children are kidnapp'd straying from their homes,
Or parted with by those who gave them birth,
Who sell their seed for lucre or from want,
And sacrifice the pledges of their love.
From the interior to the coast they come
To be transported to a distant land,
And take their leave for ever of their own.

With all that's fair to sight or memory dear :
The ties of blood, affection, friendship, love,—
The cocoa's friendly shades,—voluptuous fruits,
Delicious climate and luxurious ease,
With liberty and sunbright happiness !

In yonder cove a clipper comes to trade,
With mercenary men who cross the sea
For base degenerate purposes of gain,
And traffic in the wares of flesh and blood !
Assembled on the shore their victims stand,
Ready for transport, naked, and in chains ;
Forced by the lash to truckle to their fate,
And subject to their masters' iron will,
In a strange land, and torn from every friend,
To cultivate the soil for others' gain,
Without a chance of e'er becoming free.

In time the bonds of marriage dry their tears,
And bless them with fond pledges of their love,
Who are by heritage the masters' slaves,
And constitute the wealth of his estate.
He can dissever parent from the child,
And thus again dissolve the natural tie.
They are not prisoners of war or crime,
Nor are they monsters of the human race,

To call down vengeance on their guilty heads :
But tame and gentle, and their lot is cast
In nature's mould, without intelligence,
Spirit or power, and wear a sable skin ;
The badge of slavery and the curse of race !

The vessel's under sail with all her freight,
Cribb'd and confined like felons in their chains,
And bound they know not whither,—their long range
The open sea, blue sky, and desert air !
With little to amuse or cheer them on,
Except the stormy winds,—or distant sail,—
The dull monotony of seaboard life,—
Their own close cabin and their simple mirth,
Crowded together in contagious cells,
Half poison'd with the atmosphere they breathe.
The breeze is in the sails, and wafts them on
To distant climes, and gradually from view
They slowly dwindle to a shapeless speck,
And, sinking in the horizon, disappear !

XXIV.—(THE ROYAL CHARTER.)

A steamer, from Australia, now arrives
With a rich freight—touches the Emerald Isle,
To land some passengers, and then resumes

With joyous spirits, her expiring voyage,
With home and all its dearest ties in view!
Night hurries on and draws its shadows round;
The whistling winds in dismal voices shriek,
And swell into a tempest, rude and rough,
Driving the shrouded vessel into land
Amid the roar of breakers; tost about,
And at the mercy of the furious gale,
She leaps the angry flood, and rushes on
To her destruction: the bewildered crew
Fly to the helm, but fail to change her course;
Rockets and blue lights, hurl'd into the sky
With cannon's roar, alarm the neighbouring shore;
When suddenly she strikes upon a rock,
To all imparting an electric shock.
Roused from their cabins, instantly appear
The frighten'd passengers, in wild alarm,
In a nude state, or scantily attired,
And rushing to and fro across the deck;
They saw in each foreboding, anxious face,
So lately beaming with the smiles of joy,
The shade of death, dim, grisly, hollow-eyed!
Orders were given, and readily obey'd,
Boats lower'd, and ropes sent to the rocky beach;

But the wild billows foaming, wash'd the ship,
Which rock'd and roll'd in agonising throes,
While the fierce hurricane its thunders blew.
Alternate hope and fear flash'd in each eye,
And all were panic-struck ; confusion reign'd,
And for self preservation each prepared ;
Some to the rigging—some the o'ercrowded boat.
The capsized vessel rested on a ridge,
And pendent hung, rock'd by the wind and tide ;
When, in a moment, with an awful crash
She broke in twain, like a fell'd forest tree,
And in the whirl of waters disappear'd !

A wild despairing shriek told all was lost !
Some float awhile and to the fragments cling ;
Some swim for shore but 'gainst the cliffs are dash'd,
Wave after wave rolls headlong to the beach,
And bubble after bubble as they sink.
A minute's pause, and that impressive scene
Of struggle and of conflict pass'd away ;
The wreck was dash'd to pieces with her freight,
And few were saved to tell the dismal tale.
Friends came to seek their corpses on the shore ;
But hundreds sank, alas ! to rise no more !

XXV.—(LIFE-BOAT.)

Launch'd is the life-boat with its gallant crew,
Upon a desperate errand life to save,
Who tug the oars and struggle with the gale,
To reach the sinking bark, but make no way;
The rolling billows tossing to and fro,
And howling tempest, with o'erflowing tide,
Baffle their giant strength, and nearly swamp
With overwhelming force the struggling boat.
Oft hid from sight between the rolling waves,
Lash'd in the shrouds the weather-beaten crew
In wild despairing cries look up to heaven,
Beseeching Providence their lives to save;
Just as the life-boat nears the sinking ship,
And hurls a coil of rope to those on board,
In time to save a remnant of the crew,
Exhausted, frozen, and half starved to death.

XXVI.—(LIGHTHOUSE.)

Around this rocky isle and shallowy coast,
Humanity spreads wide its friendly light,
From sunset hour until the break of day,

And warns with buoys of treacherous rocks beneath.
Yon lofty column with its lantern tower
In the dim distance lends its hazy light,
To guide the wandering mariner to port,
And snatch him from a suicidal course :
The illuminated town peers into view,
And in a diadem of flame appears
Enthroned upon a rising ridge of rock.

XXVII.—(BURIAL OF THE DEAD.)

Sickness had laid its withering hand on one
Returning from the Cape in deep decline,
Whither he sail'd from England's humid clime
Twelve months before ; young, genial, and beloved
By a fond mother and three sisters dear,
Who hung o'er him in ominous despair,
Imprinting farewell kisses on his lips.
Salubrious was the clime, and cheered with hope
Revived his drooping spirits for a while,
And flatter'd him with promises of health,
Too soon alas ! to fade, for his disease
Had taken deeper root and hourly spread.
On board he met with sympathising friends,
Who tenderly bewail'd his early fate,

And turn'd his thoughts from this vain-glorious world,
To brighter orbs of promise in the skies.
Exhaustion told his parting hour was come,
And showed what thoughts were passing in his mind,
By souvenirs and letters left behind
For those dear friends and relatives at home,
When with a prayer that quivered on his lip,
He made his entrance to another world
With watchful heralds wafting him above.

    Next eve was his appointed burial day,
When all the crew were summon'd to the deck
To pay the last sad duties to the dead,
Where sorrowful and speechless they stand round,
Gazing upon the hammock that contains
All that was mortal of his dear remains.
O'er the ship's side and at her stern it slung,
With the black flag that flutter'd in the breeze,
During the funeral service of the dead,
Which by the captain solemnly was read ;
When wave to wave consign'd him to the deep,
Which follow'd was by the hoarse cannon's roar,
Whose solemn echos told that all was o'er !

XXVIII.—(Divers.)

A vessel with two barges by her side
At anchor lay in sight, and near the Nore,
Intent upon recovery of a wreck.
Two monster-looking figures walk the deck,
Encased in armour like gigantic men,
Who divers prove, about to be submerged
In search of treasure in the laden ship,
Which lay embedded in its trough of sand.
A diving-bell, suspended by a crane,
Hangs o'er the gunwale, with interior seats,
Into which step th' explorers of the deep,
With iron caps and clogs to sink them down,
And balance keep against the nether tide,
Who disappear beneath the wat'ry waste.
Strange singing noises as of air condensed,
Reverberate like thunder in the ear.
Through the bell's window shot a stream of light,
Which them encircle with their glassy eyes;
Through which they see all objects passing near,
And reach at twenty fathoms ocean's floor,
To gather up the spoils which scatter'd lay,

And hoist the piecemeal cargo to the shore;
With tubes and tackle they communicate
With those above who pump in vital air.
With quick despatch they ply their busy toil,
And signalling are to the surface drawn,
Watch'd by the finny race who come to spy,
The workshop there from curiosity.

XXIX.—(ELECTRIC TELEGRAPH.)

United energy with light of mind
To great inventions and discoveries lead,
And show the ingenuity of man.
All praise to the great Being who inspires
The grand conception first reveal'd to sight!
Twisted in coils of rope are veins of wire,
(The submarine conductor of the main)
Whose flash of lightning, like a meteor's blaze,
Encircling earth, the telegram conveys!
Yor battery's erected on the shore,
With scientific instruments to test
The latent sparks of the electric shock,
When spliced together are the cable ends.
Now the leviathan her anchor weighs,
And from her funnel vomits clouds of smoke,

As slowly she retires and quits the port,
And from her hold uncoils th' electric chain
That drops into the bosom of the deep
To find a rocky and uneven bed ;
But not in sleep or idleness to lie,
For thoughts and words disturb its deep repose,
And messages of hieroglyphic cast,
As to their terminus they swiftly fly,
And interchange ideas in mute reply,
From the remotest ends of ocean's shore ;
Joining the continents and isles afar,
Annihilating fleeting time and space ;
Quick'ning the revolutions of the earth,
And hastening on its journey Phœbus' car.

XXX.—(INDIA.)

The wand of magic raised up other scenes
Across the desert seas in distant climes,
Remote from Europe's green and fertile shores,
Where first the rising sun unfolds the morn,
And wakens into life the drowsy day.
An eastern empire sits enthroned in state
Magnificence : ease, luxury, and pride,
With base corruption, jealousy, and wars,

K

Have toppled India from imperial height,
And smit her to the dust and foreign rule,
A scatter'd wreck of what was once so great!

He* who came, and saw, and conquer'd her
In ancient times, and wept to conquer more,
Found her disjointed as in modern days;
When merchant princes from the British Isles,
Began to trade and settle on the land,
Which swarm'd with petty kingdoms,—tyrant rule,
Oppression, caste, and superstitious rites,
And all the dread calamities of war,
Raging between the restless neighbouring chiefs;
Invited by a friendly tribe to join,
With promises of rich reward and spoil,
The strangers lent their help against the foe;
O'ercame and conquered, and the honour shared,
With a substantial fief and wide domain.
Thus step by step they march'd to victory,
And province after province did annex,
Until the whole was grasped at and possess'd,
Reign'd over by a Christian British Queen!

* Alexander.

XXXI.—(China.)

In the same latitudes which seas divide,
Where the monsoons set in as regular
As the Nile waters in their season rise,
The flowery land of China comes in view,
Rich in her finest silk and fragrant tea.
Clothed in celestial splendour,—regal state,—
Pomp, pride, and temples, and surrounding walls;
Swarming with millions of the human race,
Shut up and isolated from the world
On which they look with ignorant contempt,
Priding themselves on their antiquity,—
Seclusion, customs, venerable laws,—
Primitive habits,—literary works,
And their divine Confucius wise and good,
A second Solomon in rolls of fame!

XXXII.—(Japan.)

Beyond these confines as we rove the seas,
Japan emerges from obscure retreat
In oriental costume, placid air,
And looks as beaming as her sunny clime.

Familiar, social, affable, and bland,
She sits supreme in dignified attire,
Willing to fraternize with other states,
And pluck a leaf of laurel from their brows.
Resign'd and happy in domestic ties,
She cultivates the arts of peace entire,
And gives to friendly intercourse her hand.

XXXIII.—(AUSTRALIA.)

Australia, with her gold discover'd mines,
Abounds in wealth, and promises to be
Renown'd in times to come; for the full tide
Of emigration populates her shores.
They thrive and multiply, and stock the land,
The wilderness and dreary solitude,
With sons of labour from the British Isles,
Who come to tame the savage and the wild;
In place of war to introduce the arts
Of social life, and civilize the earth.
Commerce and trade are agents of the scheme,
With missionary labour to fulfil
The wise decrees of Providence to man,
And solve the problem of his being here!
The last discovery lies beyond Natal,

Where brilliant diamonds glisten in the sun,
Embedded in the soil upon the shore,
Opening up fields of treasure to the sight,
With hidden wealth and fortune at command.

MUSINGS

IN

DREAMLAND.

DREAMLAND.

WHENCE come and go these phantoms of the
    brain,
Which chase each other and return again ?
They vanish with the rising orient beams,
Again to haunt us in our nightly dreams,
When folded in the lulling arms of sleep,
Absorbed and senseless in oblivion deep.
Reflected visions of a stage within,
Present to us the shadows of our kin ;
Who in life's drama played an active part,
Ere they through side scenes one by one depart :
Like apparitions of the friends we knew,
They fade away dissolving from our view.
    Traditionary legends handed down
From sire to son, are in our memories sown,
With mythic symbols of the middle age,
Ere printing's magic art mankind engage :
Till one immortal genius* gave it birth,
And scatter'd darkness from the face of earth.

* Gutenberg.

The illustrated fables still amuse,
And point their morals for our daily use.
Instill'd into our youth the nursery tale
In riper years will turn us deadly pale.
The homely proverb and the maxim short,
Contain the pith of wisdom in a thought.
We fancy by the dog's incessant roar,
We hear the bandit's footsteps at the door ;
The fireside idyl and the witches dance,
Are but the ideal fictions of romance,
Or supernatural visions of the brain ;
Which prophets conjure up, or poets feign :
These dreamy reveries reflect the past,
Cling to the present and through lifetime last.

From them astrologers their art forecast,
And counterfeited stories of the past,

The ancient prophets in their dreams unfold
The crimes of nations, and their doom foretold,
In the dire auguries which them deceived,
And the old world implicitly believed ;
Thinking they were the oracles of God,
Who secretly communed from his abode ;
And are as fortune telling bards admired,
By saints and priests who deem them all inspired.

From them astrologers their art forecast,
And counterfeited stories of the past,

Who drew their inspirations from above,
Under the auspice of all-mighty Jove ;
Interpreting by signs and symbols given,
The hidden plans of Providence and Heaven,
As taught by the Chaldaic priesthood, lights
From twinkling stars, and superstitious rites.

Next came the wandering gipsies to foretell
The unknown future by their magic spell,
Who with their sacred books from Egypt swarm,
To practise divination, with a charm
Of cunning art the future to foreshow
Your fate and fortune in the realms below ;
The crafty sybil with her oily tongue
With flattery fills the ears of all the young,
And peers inquiringly into their eyes,
Feeling their pulse like mercury to rise.

This cormorant craving of the restless mind
About the future, draws on all mankind ;
Who feel an interest in th' immortal soul,
And knowing little try to grasp the whole ;
And in a reverie they transmigrate
To regions of their everlasting state ;
When in imagination they explore
The dark invisible receding shore.

Those mythic realms we enter when we die,
Passing through Time into Eternity,
'Midst nebulæ of stars in ungauged space,
Beyond the countless systems we can trace
With telescopic glass in fields of air,
But find an open vacuum everywhere!

Fly to some hill-top,—fancy all your own,
Or dream yourself a king upon the throne;
In thought and spirit then essay to climb
The centre of the Universe sublime,
And on a seraph's outspread wings alight,
To search for boundaries of the infinite
Which us surrounds, with systems it contains,
And where the invisible Jehovah reigns!

Not to such lofty heights do we aspire,
To scan the laws of Nature's hidden sire:
The vast fields of Creation open lie
For exploration and discovery;
Where daring genius oft attempts to climb,
To reach the threshold of the vast sublime!
Where Virgil, Dante, Milton, Goethe, trod
In the great Temple of the living God,
Whose Holy Spirit's emblem'd in a shrine
All sacred held, immortal and divine!

Who has not fancied, by some influence led,
A guardian angel watching us o'erhead;
Or spirit haunting us this side the grave,
To snatch us from temptation and to save?
Or warn from danger, or for death prepare,
As of a sea storm brewing in the air?
Or earthquake's throes ere it burst into birth,
Preceded by the labour groans of earth;
To rescue from an avalanche or wave,
Or yawning gulf, and an untimely grave?
But if born under a malignant star,
Where evil genii wage eternal war,
They into their infernal lairs entice,
To plunge us in a labyrinth of vice.

In serious mood draw near and take a glance
Of one unconscious, lying in a trance;
With faculties suspended,—earth forgot,
And funeral darkness hovering round the spot.
There a somnambulist walks in his sleep,
With open eyes to take a dangerous leap.
Insensible in slumber we remain,
While under chloroform and free from pain;
Mesmeric influence holds us in a spell,
But of the demon's black art who can tell?

The clairvoyant with a supernatural sight,
Discerns what's passing in the womb of night.
To lull their senses, some narcotics try,
And to strong drinks and soothing opium fly,
To drown in pleasing dreams their memory.
Disturb'd by some imaginative power,
The brute creation slumber, dream and snore.
The chrysalis benumb'd and dormant lies,
Until matured with wings it heavenward flies ;
An emblem of the rising of the dead,
As if the vital spirit had not fled.
Two separate existences we share,
Mortal and spiritual in this world of care,
Who in the bonds of harmony unite,
Until divorced by death the soul takes flight.
Mankind must die, but shall they rise again ?
An abstruse problem unsolved must remain.
Our speculations are but mystic dreams,
And revelation's light like flashing gleams ;
Buoy'd up with hope they soar beyond the skies,
In latitudes unknown to mortal eyes.

Discount from life the passive years of sleep,
And count the average number each may keep ;
How few who've run their threescore years and ten,
Would wish their term of life renewed again !

Upon the old conditions of the lease,
With their infirmities upon th' increase ?
The simile that life is but a dream,
Is illustrated by the winding stream,
Which flows on smoothly from its rising source,
Until it joins the ocean in its course.
Some fill with horror,—some with heavenly bliss,
Here a sun landscape,—there a dark abyss ;
Once in the spell-bound arms of death-like sleep,
These magical illusions round us creep,
As if some conjurer lodged within the brain,
Like a king's jester kept to entertain.
    Unconscious slumber is a state ideal,
But when we wake we find that life is real ;
From natural causes visions may arise,
And much depends on how the casket lies :
As gloomy weather will the soul depress,
So stormy passions madden and distress ;
Fever and indigestion, and nightmare,
With images of thought alike we share ;
Anxiety of mind and nervous fear
Disturb our slumbering senses, it is clear ;
Our habits, customs, business, leave behind
Their deep impressions hoarded in the mind ;

Which reproduces them and magnifies
Their images in microscopic eyes ;
The fervid lover of his idol dreams,—
The trader of his speculative schemes,—
The miser of his gold,—the soldier war,—
The poet of his muse in heaven afar,—
The murderer of his victim, who appears
And fills his sleep with supernatural fears :
Some think these visions but a minute last,
And photographic emblems of the past.

    At midnight when the world is lock'd in sleep,
And the tower sentinels their vigils keep,
A solemn stillness without stir or sound,
As of a death-blight, reigns on all around.
Dreams are the shadows we appear to see
In playful fancy or in imagery ;
Conceal'd within the archives of the brain,
They dormant lie until revived again,
As ghosts in sympathy return to mourn
O'er the dear relics they have left forlorn,
As we in sorrow for the friends we love,
Their graves revisit, watch'd by them above.
Or to the land of shadows do they fly,
Ere entering into immortality ;

Where they with gentler spirits mix and pine,
Who tame and culture,—soften and refine ;
Till purged from sin, and penitential grown,
When through a camera paradise is shown,
As by enchantment from the shades below,
A landscape garden with its flowery show,
Of prism colours tinged with every shade,
And everlasting wreaths which never fade ;
Arcadian beauties rich with gorgeous bloom,
Scenting the amorous gale with their perfume.

These fabulous and speculative dreams,
With which the fruitful fancy nightly teems,
Entice the mind into the dark obscure,
And supernatural regions, which allure
To pry into the future,—break the seal
Of the invisible and God reveal !

Do spirits hold communion with this sphere,
And to their late companions reappear ?
When ghostly shadows visit us at night
With lingering fondness until daybreak light ?
With telegraphic speed they cross the sea,
Communicating death-news instantly ;
Some rush spontaneously into our sight,
Ghosts of another clime forgotten quite.

L

The scenes of childhood, though our eyes grow blind,
In memory live engraven on the mind;
And friendships, form'd in that dear native home,
Will oft revive where'er our footsteps roam.

Whence comes the soul? and whither does it fly?
To nether regions, or to realms on high?
Enclosed from view in its transparent shrine,
What artist can its form and sex define?
Whose image, like, and lineage below,
We picture in our minds, but nothing know?
The phœnix from its ashes pale revives,
An emblem of the soul that never dies:
Small as a glowworm with its lantern light!
Large as a giant with a sybil's sight!
Image of Deity!—the vital spark
Imprison'd in its tabernacle ark;
The leasehold tenant of the breeding brain,
Whence ideas flow from intellect's domain;
As scum and matter fly off from the sun,
And by gyrations into globes are spun,
After the lapse of ages take their place,
As independent spheres in realms of space:
Some bards imagine to prevent surprise,
'Tis watching through the caverns of the eyes.

Invisible to sight we searching find
Its local dwelling planted in the mind.
  Chameleon-like from timid fear and fright
It changes colour into blue and white.
In some 'tis languid, melancholy, sad,
And misanthropic as if going mad;
In others lively, cheerful, bright and gay,
As glowing sunshine on a summer's day:
With various faculties and genius bold,
Alike peculiar to the young and old,
Adorned with robes of elegance and grace,
It sympathizes with the human race.
If visionary we ourselves deceive;
In its existence all mankind believe,
And question not when they lie down to die,
But place their trust in immortality.
Exalted hope points to a heaven above,
And an elysium fill'd with bliss and love!
  In a deep sleep transported to the skies,
Sever'd from earth the restless spirit flies
Its fleshly tabernacle; to explore
The spangled universe and upward soar
To spectral regions in a star-lit sphere,
To catch a glimpse of those to memory dear;

While passing through the nether realms of time,
Ere winging to the heavenly and sublime!
In this my dream or stolen interview
Of kith and kin it fondly loved and knew,
Were found th' elysian fields with verdure bright,
Basking in beams of sunshine and delight;
But summoned hence by crow of chanticleer,
The startled ghosts take fright and disappear.

    Again the soul its fluttering wings expand,
And through the air alights in fairy land;
A midway orb betwixt the heavens and earth,
Where sylphs and fairies have a mythic birth,
Tossing and frisking in the cones of hay,
Where all the tiny elves in frolic play;
Where fun and laughter, merry dance and song,
And youthful pranks the festive hours prolong.
They various shapes and characters assume,
Disguis'd in masks, and in the distance loom
Like chubby cupids hovering on the wing
In the pale moonlight or the fairy ring;
Aiming their arrows at the human heart,
The bull's-eye target of their feather'd dart;
Fanning the smouldering passions into flames,
The fancy tickling with their sportive games.

Ethereal forms, light, fanciful and gay,
As represented in a comic play
Or pantomime by the enchanter's wand,
Where all the stage scenes change at his command.
Though bent with age and round with wrinkles hung,
Their philtres soon restore and make you young.
    From these enchantments which the soul entrance,
While its companion slumbers in a trance,
Forgetting all things earthly, time and race,
We fly to other spheres in depth of space;
Invisible to all of mortal mould,
And which the immortal only can behold;
Where mount Olympus with its banded guards,
Surround Parnassus and its spectral bards,
Who join their symphonies and inspired lays
In choral harmony and songs of praise,
Accompanied with instruments and lyres,
And soft delicious music that inspires.
The nine celestial Muses here preside
Over the fine arts, and are close allied
To fabled deities renown'd by name,
In heathen annals for their amorous flame,
Attended by the Graces half divine,
Whose figures through their robes of drapery shine.

These misty shadows, which like phantoms rise,
Fade and dissolve in our pictorial eyes.

From these romantic scenes and unguaged skies,
To scenes beyond my swift wing'd spirit flies,
And down the crater of a volcano,
Descends to regions dark and deep below,
Divided into chambers,—spacious halls,
Antediluvian caves and calcined walls,
With cinder ashes mixed and heaps of stones,
And extinct animals' gigantic bones ;
With scoria, pumice, bitumen and dust,
Which from its womb in conflagration burst
In streams of lava down the mountain's side,
A fiery river with a rolling tide.
A long and winding avenue branch'd near,
Which fill'd with apprehension, dread and fear.
Through gloomy vaults was heard a sullen roar
Of lashing waters on the murmuring shore,
Which proved to be the river Styx's tide,
Or waters of oblivion, which divide
Pluto's dark regions and immortal ghosts,
From mortal beings and from earthly coasts ;
Which Charon crosses with his freight of souls,
Through foaming breakers and o'er treacherous shoals,

And landing them upon the spectral shore,
Trims his broad wind-sails and returns for more.
  Met by a jailer, stern, morose, and strong,
By law appointed to conduct the throng,
To an assembly in an open court,
Where criminals in custody are brought,
Before three judges seated on a dais,
On whom with reverence the spectators gaze :
In stately wigs, silk gowns and robes of state,
With due decorum all in silence wait ;
With solemn gravity the court begins
To judge the prisoners for their earthly sins.
  According to the nature and degree
Of mortal crimes their punishment will be ;
While those who trade in slaves and levy war,
Will be confronted at that judgment bar,
And suffer all the penalties of hell,
Remorse, pain, misery, more than we can tell.
The blood-stain'd murderer and the impious mind
To solitary dungeons are confin'd,
With torture, rack, anxiety and fear,
Surpassing any martyr's sufferings here ;
Conspirators who plann'd revenge and hate,
Are sentenced to an ignominious fate ;

Condemn'd to exile in the torrid zone,
At fever heat, their vices to atone,
Or to the snowy arctic regions sent
To undergo th' extremes of punishment.
   My soul look'd on amazed at all it saw,
Somewhat resembling human courts of law :
Absorbed in meditation it withdrew,
Dodged by a phantom which it doubting knew,
In spiritual disguise, who look'd surprised,
As in its turn the stranger recognized
By dint of faculties and sense refined,
Perception keen, and intellect of mind ;
Whose graceful form and elegance perplex,
But bore the image of the gentler sex ;
Who offered escort through these regions wide
(Beset with devils) to protect and guide.
To the immortal, though not to our race,
The soul's distinguishable as the face.
They grew familiar and together walk,
Interrogating in their spiritual talk ;
And enter'd through a lodge barred with a gate,
To see fulfill'd the stern decrees of fate ;
The fiendish porter pass'd us with a scowl,
And mutter'd curses with Satanic howl.

Proud Satan, with his dark and knitted brow,
Since his rebellion rules these realms below,
The tempter and arch enemy of man,
When first created, and this globe began.

  The spirit world, from mortal eyes conceal'd,
To my dim vision was in part reveal'd;
We rambled through the windings that surround
The mazy labyrinth that lies underground,
Enclosed in Tartarus, devoid of light,
Where all is darkness and continuous night;
Enveloped in an atmosphere of gloom,
Which bore the semblance of a silent tomb.
A stifling smell of sulphur fill'd the air,
And flaming furnace lent its dazzling glare.
Scourged and confin'd within a narrow cell,
Division'd off the evil spirits dwell,
Writhing in agony, despair and fear,
Whose awful groans with terror reach the ear.
Some rave like madmen shrieking out with pain,
While others yell, reproach, and loud complain
Of mental sufferings,—cruelties refin'd,
And frightful horrors unreveal'd behind;
Where hideous furies gnash their teeth and scold,
And wither'd hags affright you to behold;

With monster demons to o'ersee the whole,
Who forge new fetters to refine the soul.
Some with uplifted hand to aching head,
Transparent look'd and tears of memory shed ;
While ruminating on the dreary past,
With sorrowful emotions overcast ;
The stings of conscience, terrible and sad,
With solitary prisons drove them mad.

These ghastly shadows with their doleful cries,
Bewail their fate in lamentable sighs ;
And legions penitential grown deplore
Their guilty deeds upon the Stygian shore,
Without a ray of hope their souls to cheer,
But a depressing, never ending fear ;
The luxury of sleep enjoy'd by men
And lower creatures is denied to them ;
The isolated miser, starving, old,
Still shows his appetite for hoarding gold :
There stumbling Sisyphus with rolling stone,
Upon the precipice comes tumbling down ;
And fainting Tantalus, about to sip
The brimful pitcher, dropp'd it from his lip.
Some hiss'd and cursed their tyrant kings by name,
Who for revenge, ambition, glory, fame,

Their armies led into the battle plain,
Strewed with the corpses of the bleeding slain ;
Upbraiding those who caused their mental woes,
They piecemeal tried to tear their spectral foes :
Dismay and terror fill'd us with alarm,
Till reassur'd that they could do no harm.
Assembled were innumerable hosts
Of saintly hypocrites and impious ghosts,
Who for their blasphemy and unbelief
Were rack'd and scourg'd in this abode of grief ;
And mothers, guilty of infanticide,
Their lustful passions sought in vain to hide.
Should sudden death despatch us to the tomb,
Without repentance, what will be our doom ?
If illness some, and some misfortune wait,
Will such relax the rigid laws of fate,
A lighter punishment awarded be
In these abodes of shame and misery ?
In mercy to the paralysed and blind,
Or idiotic and deranged in mind ?
    Appall'd they turn'd with terror and disgust,
Where none without a guide themselves dare trust,
Down subterranean passages and streets
Of prison dungeons and obscure retreats,

In these intricate windings,—when I heard,
The morning anthem of a joyous bird,
At heaven's gate trilling, and the village chimes
I fondly listen'd to in early times ;
When all my senses with a flash of light
Awoke from slumbering chains and took to flight.

THE FLOOD,

A VISION.

THE FLOOD,

A VISION.

WEARY from travel, prostrate and depress'd,
In a cool avenue I sank to rest;
The flickering twilight closed upon my eyes,
In misty shadows and in lightning skies;
Deep sleep seal'd up my faculties and sight,
Where all was hooded in the shrouds of night,
As if my soul was severed from the earth,
With dim remembrance of its mortal birth,
Or part rehears'd upon the public stage
Of busy life while on its pilgrimage.
As to a sisterhood of nuns within
The holy convent, and absolved from sin,
So from the living world was I withdrawn,
As if not of it, or of woman born.
Insensible to feeling, light, and sound,
Death's apparition loom'd on all around,
Yet in my vision I in shadow saw,
The panorama I attempt to draw.

Some glimpses flash across my feverish brain
Of rattling thunder and terrific rain,
Of lightning bursting from a stormy sky,
And roaring billows rushing mountains high ;
Of plunging headlong in the foaming deep,
Of frantic mortals roused from arms of sleep,
Of labouring at the pump,—of vessels tost,
Of mainmast falling overboard and lost ;
Of driving through the winds that rudely blow,
Of floods of waters drowning all below ;
Of firing minute signals of distress,
Of lights extinguish'd, and night's wretchedness !
Of sailors in the rigging lash'd, and cries
Which pierce the clouds, and echo through the skies ;
Of wild confusion, struggling with the gale,
Of cracking timbers, and wind-shattered sail ;
While drowsy midnight held us in the dark,
And the wild elements o'erwhelm'd our bark,
When rugged rocks tore up the nervous deck,
And dash'd our vessel to an utter wreck.

The sultry atmosphere and stifled breath
Were like a furnace, and as still as death,
An omen dire of some approaching change,
Which might the laws of order disarrange.

The sun went down in crimson flames of fire,
And roseate hues that gradually expire.
The moaning woods in foreign tongues complain,
In growling thunders or soprano strain.
The blood-red moon look'd timorous and shy,
And veil'd withdrew behind the cloud-fringed sky,
Portending some disaster to our globe,
Enclosed from sight within its vapoury robe ;
The rain descended first in gentle showers,
Increasing as the stormy tempest lours ;
The stagnant pool, which on the surface lies,
Becomes a reservoir increased in size,
Expanding till it joins the slumbering lake,
When all combine their prison chains to break ;
Then form a channel for the winding brook,
Leaping and bounding through its silvery nook,
Until it meets the river in its pride,
Which in its turn descends to oceans wide.
    In local stations 'neath the spangled sky,
The fishermen their nightly calling ply,
Where they with philosophic patience wait,
With the entangling net and luring bait,
Till break of day rewards them for their toil,
And they return to land with loads of spoil.

M

Behind a canopy of clouds, dark Night
Obscured from view the firmament of light,
Where in the broad infinity of space
The planetary systems we can trace.
The centripetal sun by nature's laws
Of gravitation, solid bodies draws,
Which in their orbits travel round the sun,
As through the seasons they their courses run,
Attended by their satellites above,
As on their axis they revolve and move ;
An universe of globes which stud the sky,
Lit up with gems of sparkling brilliancy.
  Soon loud explosions burst upon my ear,
Which fill'd the trembling soul with anxious fear,
Followed by shrieking winds and floods of rain,
By vivid lightning, and fierce hurricane ;
The Earth was darken'd, and a death-like gloom
Foreshadow'd Europe's melancholy doom ;
Electric currents on the whirlwind rode,
And roaring thunders rumble and explode,
When the constituent elements of life
Mingled together in conflicting strife.
The eddying whirlpool draws the vessel down
Into a vortex threat'ning to drown,

The treacherous waterspout o'erhangs the sea,

In spiral form, and looks mysteriously.

Immersed, our planet reel'd as it turn'd round,

While plunging like a floating buoy half drown'd,

Beneath the waters reeling to and fro,

Struggling in anger 'midst the overflow ;

Heaven's windows open'd, and the floodgates burst,

Swelling the rivers' open mouths at first,

Then inundating the dry land and shore,

With all the docks and merchandise in store.

The old and new world, land and sea, change place,

With no connecting link or guide to trace ;

The floating fragments, scatter'd far and wide,

Were carried out to sea at turn of tide,

With drifting corpses mid the general wreck,

And broken remnants of a mast or deck :

Press'd on by thousands crowding close behind,

O'er the white breakers, ruffled by the wind,

Increased in volumes by the rising tide,

Upon whose back sea gulls and cormorants ride.

Since the last flood, five thousand years ago,

There had not been so vast an overflow,

Which drown'd the world, save Noah in his ark,

And those who in his wooden walls embark.

So dissolution seem'd to be at hand,
When this flood raged immersing all the land,
O'erspread the continent and highest peaks,
With lamentations, dying groans, and shrieks.

 Neptune's supremacy ruled wind and tide,
And with his trident land and sea divide;
The British Isles were flooded far and near,
And one by one began to disappear:
The tidal sea submerg'd the Goodwin sands,
And overwhelm'd the banks of other lands,
As in the channel of the Dover straits,
Whose snow white cliffs match with the Calais gates,
Which former earthquakes severed into two,
Admitting the broad ocean's passage through.
Since then convulsions parted land and main,
All tempest-torn and drown'd in floods of rain:
No earthly power could the invasion stay,
And everything in turn became its prey;
Cities and towns were swallow'd up and gone,
And now despairing men began to mourn;
The arch destroyer death was at their feet,
And they sought refuge in some cave's retreat;
All was confusion, noise, and rabble rout,
With order and authority shut out;

Trade was suspended,—all were unemploy'd,
And precious life and property destroy'd;
Each in his humour did as he inclined,
Without the pole-star of a leading mind,
And sought his own and nearest kin to save,
For thousands daily met a wat'ry grave.

As in the earth's beginning chaos rose
From elements into convulsive throes,
Formless and void ere into sphere was spun,
In darkness sunk obscured without a sun,
All in disorder, jumbled, rent, and torn,
An undigested mass when it was born,
And its adhesive properties combin'd,
Or life and motion into being join'd;
Long ere gigantic mammoths prowl'd the earth,
Or prehistoric man sprang into birth.

The Emerald Isle was rudely struck and tost,
Shaken to its foundation and nigh lost,
Leaving its boggy swamps and spongy mire,
When decomposed for fuel, peat and fire;
The channel islands next decrease in size,
As the advancing waves surround and rise,
Leaving their spiral peaks or hill-crown'd wood,
As landmarks to point out where cities stood;

Such as the garden of the Isle of Wight,
A gem of ocean partly hid from sight,
Or stormy Mona's green and fertile shore,
O'errun with Druids in the days of yore,
Whose scatter'd monuments and temples round
With sacrificial altars rude are found.
Jersey and Guernsey, with the Hebrides,
All disappear'd beneath th' invading seas,
With Gibraltar off the Spanish coast,
Malta, Madeira, Holland, and a host
Were blotted from the map and lost to view,
With their inhabitants except a few;
Fog darkness brooded o'er a sinking world,
And its last stratum into air was hurl'd,
Till chaos and confusion spread around,
And three-fourths of it overwhelmed and drown'd.
  The people saw and trembled at the sight,
And into the interior fled with fright,
Some to the lofty tops of mountains flew,
Where Nevis, Snowden, Skiddaw, rose in view,
All panic-stricken they look'd pale and wild,
And in despair the mother kiss'd her child,
Her dumb-struck partner look'd them in the face,
And sighing clasped them in a fond embrace:

Cathedral churches to their centres shook,
And theatres late crowded were forsook,
With pleasure, gaiety, amusement, mirth,
And all the vain frivolities of earth;
State palaces and castles built of stone,
Were rased to their foundations and o'erthrown,
While lofty pillars seem to float on high,
On the flood's margin near the murky sky,
Mid towers and spires and monuments of state,
Erected to the memories of the great;
These spectral ruins of departed worth,
Like beacons from their mountain tops look forth.
Kings, statesmen, warriors, nobly born and bred,
From their domains and country mansions fled,
Hills were developed on its upper crust,
And on the mountain's brows volcanos burst.
Their peaks half hidden in the jet-black clouds,
Where are assembled agitated crowds,
Seen in the distance struggling to mount higher,
Out of the reach of the volcanic fire;
And streams of boiling lava rushing o'er,
Midst clouds of smoke and thunder's awful roar;
The yawning craters liquid flames upthrew,
And ashes, smoke and dust in columns flew;

The rushing fluid lit up all the sky,
And rain'd down stones and scoria from on high,
Upon the villages around its base,
Whose entomb'd dwellings underneath you trace,
Which shared the sudden and disastrous fate
Of two lost cities of anterior date.*

Attracted by the moon the wave-tides swell,
And subterranean earthquakes rose and fell,
The earth vibrated like a cromlech-rock,
And bellow'd loud at each returning shock;
Deep in its bowels, gaseous currents pent,
Burst through the chasm struggling to find vent,
Which split up its foundations with a roar,
That echoed like artillery round the shore,
Its base upheaving into fragments torn,
With public buildings swallow'd up and gone,
Burying alive those hurrying to and fro,
As in a wreck or avalanche of snow,
Who sleep in silence in one common grave,
Now sunk beneath the rolling ocean's wave.
Oft in the rivers as they onward sail,
Some floating fragments told the withering tale.

The universal deluge swept away
The sacred relics of a former day,

* Pompeii and Herculaneum.

With antique monuments and works of art,
Preserved with reverence which touch'd every heart ;
Their household gods, and everything held dear,
Were now abandoned with a silent tear,
With precious jewels,—ornaments of gold,
Reflecting mirrors,—relics choice and old,
Point lace, embroidery and china ware,
With statuary unique, and paintings rare.

The haunts of men were silent as the grave,
All ridden o'er by each returning wave ;
The seats of learning and the courts of law,
The legislature, halls, exchange and spa,
Where congregated thousands used to meet
At exhibitions, balls, and public street ;
All were deserted or in ruins laid,
And all their household pets crouch'd down dismay'd ;
The faithful dog, domestic cat, and bird,
Were paralyzed, and not a sound was heard.
When this calamity was at its height,
A venomous disease appeared in blight,
Plague, cholera and small pox, spread and grew,
Impregnating the air, and thousands slew,
Adding fresh sorrow to the general gloom,
And hurrying its victims to the tomb.

The bridge, the tower, the telegraph and rail,
Deserted told their melancholy tale,
Friends sympathize with friends with sorrowing heart,
Then bid farewell for ever and depart
They know not whither, with a wail and cry,
E'en as a starving animal to die.
Relinquish'd by their tenants who took flight,
The empty houses were a sorry sight,
For they were wreck'd and plunder'd, and despoil'd
Of their contents, for which their owners toil'd.
The watchful dog, his master's pet and pride,
Licking his hand, laid down and sobb'd and died;
The fiercer animals roared out with rage,
But hunger tamed them in their iron cage;
Wild beasts were terrified and found a grave
Within the deep recesses of a cave,
Whose huddled bones in after times are found,
To testify the brutal races drown'd.
Abandon'd ships lay rotting in the sea,
And frowning icebergs float majestically,
In boats provision'd, some set sail for France,
Some to the channel isles to take their chance;
Lost in mid ocean they could not be found,
And most, as if they had not been, were drown'd;

Some to the Mediterranean isles of Spain,
Accompanied with thunder clouds and rain,
Or the peninsular and isles remote,
Which look'd like spectral ruins all afloat;
The tides set in throughout the Pyrenees,
And swamp'd them all in the encroaching seas;
By currents driven into Biscay's bay,
The billowy ocean seized upon its prey,
Then overran the lofty Alpine chain,
Which riven asunder had for ages lain;
Whose tops and domes look'd floating in the skies,
As the all-swelling roaring waters rise;
Others to German ports, and some to Rome,
But all regretted they had left their home:
The ocean grappled with the land for place,
And Europe sunk, you could no longer trace.
Lighthouses were abandon'd or blown down,
That warn'd from nether rocks, and lit the town;
Corpses were strewn on every strand and shore,
And every tide-wave wash'd up hundreds more,
With some dear pledge of love around the neck,
Or finger-ring snatch'd from the general wreck,
Or miniature recalling some one dear,
Embalm'd in memory with a silent tear,

Whose scatter'd fragments in disorder lay,
The spoil of lifeless cities in decay.

   The origin of this disastrous flood
From natural causes sprang and not from God,
Who once repented in its early birth,
He had destroy'd his children of the earth ;
Beneath whose crust descending we explore,
And find the coal-fields, and the mineral ore,
But speculate in fancy of the core ;—
Through different strata calculate its age,
And theorize on each successive stage.
The adit entering, we undermine
With blasts of powder the metallic mine,
Heaving ourselves a passage to the vein
We follow, where for ages it had lain,
In dark unfathomable depths below,
Disturb'd by forces or an overflow ;
Through passages and halls we wend our way,
Below the surface from the light of day,
To dismal regions where bright torches flare,
Which o'er the human visage throws a glare
Of ghastly paleness, and the glassy eye,
Which look so many demons standing by,
Who burrow in the earth from year to year,
Without a ray of sunshine them to cheer,

And in relays lit by the flickering light,
Pursue their labours, morning, noon, and night.

The elemental strife gave warning note,
In grating thunder and in wrecks that float,
Encroaching and engulphing all the coast,
With rolling waves and hurricanes that tost :
The angry surges rose up mountains high,
Lash'd into fury by the tempest nigh.
Though hourly watch'd, the overwhelming tide,
No flattering promise gave it would subside,
Alarm and fear in every face were read,
And through the towns and villages were spread,
Mines were forsaken, and a panic ran
From house to house, and spread from man to man ;
Children were frighten'd ;—mothers in despair
Like maniacs raved, and wildly tore their hair.
For consultation groups assembled round
The dying embers of the smoking ground,
And ever and anon with fuel fed
The flickering flame that gather'd o'er its head ;
Deranged, the angry strife spread far and wide,
And tens of thousands of starvation died,
Their crops were rotted and their stores destroy'd,
And all the peasantry quite unemploy'd.

Man's vices and his passions were subdued,
As want increased his appetite for food,
Disease with pestilence and famine reign,
While other miseries follow'd in the train ;
In place of order, wild disorder grew,
Till man the christian became savage too ;
When in fraternal bonds mankind unite
For preservation, law, and equal right,
Which cheered alike the powerful and the weak,
And brought a transient rainbow to the cheek.
Mental affliction on his senses seiz'd,
And insane actions show'd a mind diseased,
Contagious war with neighbouring nations ceased,
As the all-conquering elements increased,
Diminishing in numbers which o'erran
Th' inferior creatures, and the tribes of man.

Death and destruction stared around and spread,
And from impending fate and ruin fled,
All undetermined which way they should go,
Out of the reach of the invading foe ;
Friend clung to friend and families unite,
For none could safety see except in flight ;
Some hugg'd the land, while others put to sea,
To take their chance and rush on destiny,

Till most were scatter'd from their island home,
The broad and liquid elements to roam.
Some destitute of rudder, compass, sail,
In latitudes where angry winds prevail,
Take the bright pole-star for their trusted guide,
As o'er the wreathed wave they onward ride,
Meeting terrific icebergs in the pack,
Piled to the heavens upon the ocean's back;
The drift of ages centred round the pole,
A belt of ice encompasseth the whole
Muttering hoarse thunder as they split and break,
With trembling motion, and electric shake,
Where everlasting snow attires the ground,
And on whose shores eternal winter's found.

The grass-green rollers of the Baltic wave
Swept mariners by hundreds to their grave.
The hardy veteran who knew no fear,
And underwent sea dangers all the year,
Exposed to storms and tempests, look'd aghast,
As he survey'd the havoc from the mast,
Expecting every hour would be his last;
For broken fragments floated all around,
With merchandise and corpses of the drown'd;
Dismasted vessels felt the withering shock,
As they, unmann'd, were dash'd against the rock;

Abandon'd by their crews some craft caught fire,
Burn to the water's edge and then expire:
No desperate pirate roam'd the sea's highway,
In ambush hid to pounce upon his prey;
No smuggler's beacon warn'd of dangers near,
Or coastguard men, or channel fleet to fear;
No sordid slaver to kidnap the child,
And drive the broken-hearted mother wild;
No trader to exchange his wares for gold,
Or glutted markets where all stores were sold;
Suspense o'erawed, and panic seized them all
Without distinction between great and small.

   The rumbling air was fill'd with doleful cries
Of screaming eagles as they heavenward rise,
And the wild condor as it takes its flight
On wings extended beyond reach of sight;
The ravenous vulture scents his carrion food,
And gluts his appetite with flesh and blood;
The cormorants chase those who 've gone astray,
And pouncing down, seize and devour their prey;
The hawk and falcon, train'd in days gone by
With lures and sports to gambol in the sky,—
The sea-gull dives beneath the foaming crest,
Or lights upon the vessel's mast for rest.

While small and timid birds cling to the wreck,
Or frighten'd drop exhausted on the deck.

While thus the elemental strife made head,
And chaos and confusion widely spread,
Leviathans and monsters of the deep
In great commotion out the ocean leap ;
Beneath the billows, shoals of fishes roam
In depths unfathom'd and to man unknown ;
Various in nature, body, form, and size,
With fins to swim and float, descend and rise ;
The bulky tail of the gigantic whale
Serves for a rudder, instrument and sail ;
The ravenous shark's an enemy to all
Who dive beneath, and preys on great and small ;
The dolphin, grampus, porpoise meet the eye,
With turbot, salmon, cod, and smaller fry.

Columbus open'd up a continent,
And thither to America some went,
Abandoning the old world for the new,
And sigh'd and sobb'd while taking their adieu
Of fond and fair ones on the parting shore,
Who felt they should each other see no more,
Spontaneous kisses met the lips and face,
While tenderly repeating the embrace.

The bell had toll'd its last, its hurrying peal,
The anchor's weigh'd, and steersman at the wheel,
A wail, a shriek has wrenched their arms apart,
But not dissolved the union of the heart;
The fading vessel's watch'd till out of sight,
And those on land until the fall of night;
Till not a speck remained on either side
The hemisphere, to show they were allied;
When weary watching lulls them into sleep,
As they in broken slumbers cross the deep.

 Each day's monotony of sea and sky
Grew tedious to the unfamiliar eye,
Some to beguile the time, employ the mind
In reading, writing, and amusement find.
To Newfoundland they first direct their course,
Or stretch their canvas to some nearer source,
Such as the States where emigration's tide
Set in from Europe's shores and multiplied,
Where hostile tribes of savages abound,
Engaged in deadly feud with all around.
The scatter'd wanderers left their seed behind,
And dared the ocean with its storms and wind;
Sprung from our loins, the adventurous few
Increased in number and to empire grew.

The equinoctial gales and fierce typhoon,

Blow loud and clamorous as the trade monsoon;

The blusterous winds of March are rude and gruff,

Though viewless to the sight and tempest rough.

Dispirited by suffering and despair,

To the new world some emigrants repair;

Reduced to biscuits, the half famished crews,

'Tween death and casting lots began to muse,

To eke out life unto its widest span,

And feast like cannibals on fellow man;

Who hour by hour keep anxious watch, but fail

To see a speck enlarging to a sail;

The foaming cataracts came leaping o'er

The rocky precipice with thundering roar,

The steamer from beneath received a shock,

And drove with fury on a sunken rock,

While bark and schooner, with their mast and sail,

Were in collision driven by the gale,

And from their hammocks roused the slumbering crew,

Who to the deck by sudden instinct flew,

In time to see the vessel (none could save)

Plunge with a groan beneath the yeasty wave,

Which toss'd the passengers into the sea,

Amongst the breakers shouting piteously;

Till one by one they sank and rose again,
Swimming and struggling till but few remain,
Who saved themselves by clinging to the wreck,
Upon the floating hull, or mast and deck.

EPITAPHS.

I

How soothing and how sacred 'tis to pause
  Upon the memory of those we love;
To reconcile our grief with Nature's laws,
  Resigned to think that we shall meet above!

II

Dissolved is every earthly tie,
  Which link'd her Spirit here;
Her future is Eternity,
  Where all are drawing near.

III

Within the compass of a circling year,
How many dear beloved ones disappear!
Miss'd from the family of social life,
Child, father, mother, sister, brother, wife;—
Creates a desert,—leaves a blank behind,
With many a broken heart and shipwreck'd mind.

IV

The spring time of youth is seen passing away,
Like the orb in the west at the close of the day;
The earth is in motion,—the heavens are in sight,
But soon are obscured like the visions of night!
Vast empires which flourish'd long ages ago,
With their kings and their conquerors, where are they
    now?
The greatest of nations since then have had birth,
And cities built up at the confines of earth.
The ruin which tells of the havoc of time,
Recalls back a period when first in its prime.
All things tell of change from the seed to the tree,
The convulsions of Nature in mountain and sea!
How various the seasons of youth up to age!
How capricious the actions of man on the stage!
The down of his head, and decay of his mind,
Show his march to be onward with mile-stones behind;
And the swift wings of Time, with the mould of decay,
Prove man to be changing and passing away!

V

If guardian angels from above,
Descend to watch o'er those they love;

How eager they must be to see
The suffering soul from bonds set free !

How soothing to th' afflicted here,
For whom no cure but death is near,
Peacefully to lie down and die,
Assured of Immortality !

SONNET TO HOPE.

Inspiring Hope, thy smiles illume the mind,
   And mould us for the world in which we live;
   In realms of fancy thou canst pleasure give,
The brightest flatterer that we here can find,
For to the fruitful mother thou art kind,
   And to the lover, or the fugitive,
   A pictured Paradise in which they live:
The shipwreck'd mariner on shore confin'd,
   The martial soldier's warm inspiring friend:
While breath is in the dying there lives hope,
And genius budding has thy telescope;
   The pious souls of earth on Heaven depend;
To thee we look like children to a mother,
In thee we find a friend when we've no other!

PARODY ON HAMLET'S SOLILOQUY.

To rhyme or not to rhyme, that is the question :—
Whether 'tis nobler in the mind to endure
The spleen and venom of ill-temper'd men,
Or to take arms against the tribe of critics
And by opposing conquer ? to write,—to rhyme,—
No more ; and by oblivion say we shun
The head and heart-ache, and the thousand ills
Poetic flesh is heir to ;—'tis a consolation
Devoutly to be wish'd.   To sing ;—to rhyme ;—
To rhyme ! perchance in doggrel ; ay, there's the rub,
For in that tide of thought what fame may come,
When we have run the lease of four score years,
Must give us pause. There's the reward,
If present fortune disappoint the bard
That spurs ambition in the minstrel's breast :
For who would bear the toil and sweat of years—
The rivalship of bards,—satiric censures,
The pangs of study, restlessness of thought,—

The insolence of rivals, and the shafts
Of envy,—the jest and slander of the world;
When one might these vexatious troubles shun
By being mute? who would satire bear,
And live a solitary weary life;
But that the wish of something after death,
Fame, honour, glory, may triumphant rise,
To crown the poet's manes,—puzzles the will;
And makes us rather bear besieging ills,
Than shun ambition and immortal fame?
Thus hope's the anchor to which authors cling;
And thus a fix'd and steady resolution
Buoys up inspiring courage—prompts the mind
To enterprizes of great deeds and moment,
From this side scene the mystery subsides,
And musing poets warble.

ON LEAVING TOWN FOR THE COUNTRY.

LAST summer found me in the west,
And Devon owned me for a guest :
Now newly fledg'd I issue forth
To the cold regions of the north.
Across the rough capricious sea,
Lie scenes of curiosity ;
The sacred relics of an age
But briefly chronicled in page
Of history, and ruins grey,
O'er which Time's shadows lingering stray,—
Or towering mountains piercing through
The mists that curtain up heaven's blue,—
The amber stream o'er rocky bed,
The waterfall from mountain's head,
The fertile valleys rich and green,
Smiling upon the sylvan scene,—
The crystal lake's unruffled breast,
Encircled in its sylvan nest,—

And landscape scenery around
In foliage clad, will there be found!
Turn we to them, and loose the mind
From chains of slavery left behind.

THE DISAPPOINTED AUTHOR.

Each age has its peculiar tide,
Of thought and feeling, which divide
And waft us from the grave to gay,
From sullen night to cheerful day ;
While o'er the mind these meteors stealing,
Inspiring with the rays of feeling,
And fancy soaring on her wings,
The minstrel meditates and sings.
With music in his soul and eye,
He weaves delicious harmony,
When inspiration strings his lyre
And wraps his soul in flames of fire ;
And brilliant thoughts flow into rhyme,
As bells harmoniously chime,
And silver sounds of music sips
Like honey from the ruby lips,
Of that half mortal,—half divine
Being of love, who charms like wine.

Oh! I've felt the kindling flame
In my breast, and sigh'd for fame.
Fancy on her pinions soaring,
Sets my lofty soul exploring:
Up the archway of the sun,
My Pegasus has bravely run,
And prostrate pray'd the gifted Nine,
To let my lamp of genius shine.
But the nymphs refuse to smile
On my flowrets yet awhile;
Pilgrim-like I must retire
From the town to tune my lyre,
Ere the Muses will inspire.

Though Envy casts her jealous eye,
And all the curs beneath the sky
Conspire their favour to refuse
For having taken up the Muse,
Still let them rave, lash, and dissect
This image, and that rhyme reject,
They shall not sting me with their ire,
For I'm apprenticed to the lyre.
Too prone to censure and to blame,
They ridicule and blast your fame;
It is their nature and their trade:
(What will not critics do if paid?)

I care not to provoke their rage,
For every line they'll give a page,
With rancour, hatred, poison fill'd,
From senseless muddy brains distill'd.
These brutal pirates of the press,
Rob, plunder, castigate, distress,
All who may chance to cross their way,
For all alike to them are prey,
Save those who purchase with a bribe
The pens of the reviewing tribe.

    Fondly attach'd to solitude
I gladly would myself seclude
In sylvan glades from vulgar sight,
To meditate away the night,
And wed the Muse of sacred song,
To whom the sweetest airs belong;
For few there are more prone to fly
From city hum, and Plutus' eye,
For nature's charming, quiet spot,
To be oblivious and forgot!

EPITAPH ON ONE BORN AT SEA.

I WAS not born a child of earth,
But Venus-like received my birth
'Neath crystal chambers of the sea,
'Midst monsters who surrounded me.
The billows bore me on their backs,
And lodged me safe from rude attacks
In a wall'd cradle of the ocean,
Rock'd by the winds and waves in motion,
Which lull'd me in oblivious sleep,
In a wing'd ship that plough'd the deep :
And then was cast upon the shore
Like Jonah, own'd by none, and poor ;
Where after wandering awhile,
A stranger in this sea-girt isle,
Without a country, home, or friend
To claim me, or on whom depend,
Death pass'd me in my virgin bloom,
An infant orphan to the tomb !

FRAGMENT.

THE KING OF CHEROKEE IN THE COUNCIL CHAMBER,
SOLILOQUISING BEFORE BATTLE.

THE storm is gathering fast;—on yonder hill
The native tribes of warriors will meet,
And men with men do battle like wild beasts,
And thousands like tall cedars be hewed down;
Imagination, visions, streams of blood,
And heaven itself portends with awful signs;
For now the waning moon so crimson red,
Looks down in threat'ning wrath upon the field,
And blazing comets cross the troubled sky,
With shooting stars, the messengers of death!
The thirsty ground will quench itself with blood,
And drink and fatten on the tide of life
That courses through these veins and bleeding
        heart!—
This hamlet will be flooded with our gore,
And nourish'd with our bleach'd and scatter'd bones;

For if I live not free, I cease to live!
And mother Earth must find her son a grave!
　Now let us arm ourselves against the foe,
And gratify our passion for revenge,
And dip our poison'd arrows in their blood,
And drive them backward in the raging sea.
Now let the war-whoop sound their funeral knell,
And free our country from these pale-faced men,
Brace every sinew to the sticking place.
Fear not their fiery weapons,—let their thunder
Be music to our ears to spur us on
To victory or death, rather than be slaves
And subject to their chains and iron rule!
　Hosts have been scatter'd,—villages burnt down,
Wives become widows,—children orphans left;
Like forests 'fore the blast our heroes fell!
Ungrateful, treacherous, hypocrites of hell!
Their heads are pregnant with the ill designs
Of their ambition, too deep for common thought;
Their appetite increases with their food,
And we must quell the rage of't, or be slaves!
Success produces tyranny and pride:
We gave them much, but they've exacted more!
We thought them tame, but they have proved them
　　wild!

Like locusts have they plagued the land and sea,
Spreading fierce desolation all around,
Till all the tribes for vengeance cry aloud.
Our property is plunder'd,—food destroy'd,
By these marauders landing on our coast,
And all that we hold dear, and cherish most
Of family connection,—ties of love
Are sacrificed in common to their lust
And selfish avarice, which if gratified
With the whole world, would covet stars above!
　　The spirits of our fathers call on us,
The ashes of their bodies to protect
From sacrilege!—dance on,—prepare for fight!
For we'll dispute our country.inch by inch,
And lay the proud usurper at our feet,
We'll battle on till they shall disappear,
And fly for safety in their ships at sea!

A SKETCH.

ROMANTIC days of chivalry are o'er,
   And with them half the glory of the brave;
For tournaments and jousts are now no more,
   With restless spirits who were wont to rave
And sell their lives for freedom, but to claim
A never dying monument of fame.

But now that they are in oblivion cast,
   We look and pause on them with lingering eye,
As on the visionary youthful past
   Through a long vista,—things that have gone by:
And all absorb'd in fancy's mazy dream,
Briefly forget we 're on life's rapid stream.

Their warlike spirits fill'd the ranks of war,
   Inspiring with their deeds the valorous heart;
And the brave chief shone like a glittering star
   Amid his satellites; does to them impart

Heroic courage both by word and deed,
And in the heat of battle thousands bleed.

Dreadful the carnage of one fearful night,
    When the full moon survey'd the battle field,
And the red pool bore witness to the fight,
    Where the strewn heaps of wreck lay unconceal'd :
The atmosphere was tainted with the dead,
So many legions for their country bled.

Some heartless monsters, by base lucre led,
    Stole out of camp from dusk till break of day,
To plunder the expiring and the dead,
    As on the blood-stain'd ground they weltering lay ;
They pass from man to man o'er hills of slain,
And stab to death the groaning who complain.

Next morn the bursting sun rose in a haze
    From out the bosom of the boisterous deep,
But, as he rises, crimsons and surveys
    That scene of horrors where the victims sleep ;
Stricken with awe, he clouds himself on high,
Like a veil'd mourner grieving in the sky.

The victor was not there, where all was gloom,
  And birds of prey were fattening on the dead;
But there was one emerging from the tomb,
  A pale-faced spectre with a bleeding head;
No drink was nigh to quench his burning thirst,
His sicken'd heart felt faint, and pants to burst.

No cry for help,—no death-groan reach'd his ear,
  A midnight silence reign'd on all around;
Half raised, he wildly stared, and dash'd a tear,
  Then closed his eyes, and sank upon the ground
To breathe and then expire;—the vital spark
Forsook the lamp, and left him in the dark.

———————

TO MY ABSENT WIFE.

HAIL! lady of the house at home,
We urge and welcome you to come;
Your absence, like the shrouded sun,
Gives ennui to more than one,
For parrot, puss and singing bird,
Mope all day long without a word;
The servants too look out of tune,
And hope you'll be returning soon,
To cheer them with your spirits bright,
And turn their dullness into light,
As does the sun its satellite.

As for myself, bereft, alone,
It is monotonous I own;
Companionship since we were wed,
Is look'd for as my daily bread;
To see thee and to hear thy voice,
Unfits me for this sham divorce.

However studiously inclined,
Thy image flits before my mind,
And thence finds entrance to my heart,
As if it were a counterpart.
To fill up time I write and read,
Ride, garden, visit, walk and feed.
My vacant leisure to amuse,
I oft invoke the sacred Muse,
And in my dreams of fancy view
A pastoral nymph resembling you,
Beneath some tree's umbrageous shade,
Where once her piping shepherd play'd.

When peaceful slumbers me invite
To pass away the tedious night,
Then restless thoughts on various themes
Disturb my train of hideous dreams;
Sprites, goblins, fairies, crowd my brain,
And rouse but cannot lull again:
I twist and turn from side to side,
And half my thoughts with you divide.
Then while the mists enfold our sphere,
And darkness fills with nervous fear,
Fatigued, exhausted and depress'd,
I sink into oblivious rest,

To wake with the return of morn
And consciousness, as newly born;
Then after haunting all night through,
Your face again peers into view.

If to see an old relation,
Leaves a void in our creation,
What if foreign climes should sever
And dissolve our tie for ever?
Or either should succumb to fate,
And leave the other desolate?
The world would be a blank and shade,
And dreary life decline and fade.

ON WITNESSING MR. YOUNG'S 'HAMLET'.

His melancholy aspect, piercing eye,
And cloudy thoughts that prey upon his reason,
Bespeak the agitation of his soul
And bosom's anguish. The usurper's voice,
Like poison in the ear, stirs in his brow
The frowns of indignation and revenge:
Suspicion lurks in his distemper'd brain,
And deep dejection settles on his cheek:
He mourns and feels the pangs of madness, while
Reflecting on the frailty of his mother,
Until his swelling heart could burst with grief,
Or he himself dissolve away to tears !
Alone he follows his poor father's ghost
(Though danger threatens, and his friends dissuade),
Through all the windings of the mazy wood,
And bends with anxious eye and list'ning ear,
To hear the tale that harrows up his soul,
Curdles his blood, and all his senses steals:

He breathes his lamentations with a sigh
That rushes from the fountain of despair,
In the dark prison of his padlock'd mind,
Thirsting for vengeance. Half resolved to die,
And end the thousand ills of suffering life,
He stops to pause if ills with life expire?
And finds 'tis better to endure them still,
Than fly to others that we dream not of.

His scheme, the play, disquiets king and queen,
Who're frighten'd with the represented death,
Which stings their conscience,—awes their troubled
   minds,
And proves them guilty of th' unnatural crime.

Oh! who has heard, can e'er forget the son
The queen upbraiding with the blackest sin,
Hurling ten thousand daggers to her heart,
In words which sink into her haughty soul
Like death news from the shadowy Stygian shore,
Giving to bitter thoughts the worst of pangs,
Which fill the mind with terror and despair.

With what philosophy,—abstracted mind,
He treats the clay-cold soil of human flesh,
And moralizes o'er the wrecks of time,

With hallow'd feeling towards the senseless skulls,
Thrown from the bony grave with humorous jest,
Recalling Yorick from long years of sleep,
While gazing on his hideous, eyeless skull !

H Y M N.

PRESIDING Spirit! 'tis to thee
We come with offerings of prayer
And heartfelt praises, when we see
Thy blessings scatter'd everywhere.

Watch me guardian angels, watch me,
From thy heavenly sphere above;
Guide me, shield me, bless and help me,
Through my pilgrimage, and love.

If paternal love endears us,
And we're thought of in the skies,
Disunited, they will cheer us
With our own begotten ties.

In remembrance we will hold them
Ever present to our sight;

In our visions we behold them,
   Spirits of seraphic light.

If transparent forms of being,
   Sensitive with vital breath,
They are gifted with soul-seeing,
   Far beyond the gates of Death.

If oblivious and ethereal,
   They forget the things of earth;
They appear to us ideal
   In their disembodied birth.

Flitting shadows, round us winging,
   Seem the angels once we knew,
And the distant voices singing
   Into whispers died and flew.

TO E.

Accept this album from a friend,
    As token of a love sincere ;
In memory keep it to life's end,
    In proof you hold the giver dear.

Amongst the photographs you'll find
    Our dearest kin in every page ;
And others will be brought to mind,
    While actors on life's busy stage.

If living, underwrite the name,
    If past away, add age and date,
That friends, while musing o'er the same,
    May read a lesson in their fate.

Preserved in memory, the best
    Still visit us from yonder skies ;

One touch of nature in the breast
   Their image brings before our eyes.

Assembled here the good and great
   In this small gallery of art,
Will be remember'd as the late,
   And find a niche in every heart.

If changed in likeness, form and face,
   By absence in a foreign clime,
In after years we only trace
   The ruins of departed Time.

If we their chronicles review,
   And into parts divide the whole;
How swift th' electric flashes flew
   Along the wire from pole to pole!

All human life is but a span,
   When measured by Time's yearly glass:
The boy has grown into a man,
   For whom the sands too quickly pass.

209

TO-MORROW.

WHAT will to-morrow's post bring here ?
A sunbright joy, or dew-drop tear,
Trickling through fissures, drop by drop,
From hidden springs or mountain top ?

To-morrow's telegraph will bring
Swift Mercuries upon the wing,
With news from foreign countries wide,
Through wiry cables 'neath the tide.

The daily papers come to hand,
With latest tidings of the land,
Spreading sensational surprise,
When an enlighten'd genius dies.

Life is an emblem of to-day ;
To-morrow creeps but fades away,

P

And like the mirage floats before,
On an imaginary shore.

The opening of a brilliant morn
Proclaims another day is born ;
But, like a shadow on the wall,
To-morrow never comes at all,

But lags behind the light of day,
Masking its face as yesterday,
And steals upon us at midnight,
But ne'er reveals itself to sight.

To-morrow may, if summon'd hence,
Find us deprived of every sense ;
Cold as an effigy of stone,
When our immortal spirit's flown,

THE KISS.

Gift of angels from above,
　To the gentler sex was given,
As a pledge of faith and love,
　With a contract seal'd in heaven.

If on earth there's pictured bliss,
　'Tis a mother's fond embrace,
When she prints the rapturous kiss
　On the miniatured one's face.

When our bright ones rush in sight,
　With their smiles and joyous bounds,
Grasping hands and lips unite
　With a peal of merry sounds.

When the sun sets deep in heaven,
　And for slumbers you prepare,
The sweet parting kiss is given,
　With a blessing and a prayer.

When in youth the virgin's blush
　　Hangs like fruit upon the tree,
Banquet on that crimson flush,
　　'Tis like nectar of the bee.

When true lovers first admire,
　　And love kindles into flame,
'Tis not passionate desire,
　　But a transport none can tame.

This inspires the throbbing breast
　　With an amorous delight:
Flying homeward to their nest,
　　They like turtle doves unite.

When belov'd ones emigrate
　　To a distant foreign shore,
Fond and full hearts cling and break,
　　For they may not see him more.

When we take the last farewell
　　Of our friends and kindred dear,
An impressive kiss will tell
　　Our emotion in a tear.

LONDON.

WEALTHIEST of cities, paragon of sights,
Birthplace of freedom and of charter'd rights,
Whose origin and progress we can trace
Through the dim annals of our ancient race,
Where Rome's invading legions put to rout
The natives rude, and drove the Britons out!
Ancestral blood diluted you may trace
In Danish, Saxon, and the Norman race,
Now counterfeited in the English face.
Here the imperial court resides and draws,
And senates meet to rectify our laws,
Where brilliant eloquence and wisdom soar,
The classic realms of genius to explore;
A noble river with its flowing tides
Winds through the city, and its shores divides,
And join'd by granite bridges which expand,
Look ornamental, elegant, and grand!
Church-spires and towers meet in the smoky skies,
And monuments to memory arise.

The old cathedrals, raised in popish days
Receive our admiration and our praise;
Their venerable look,—exalted height,
Inspire respect and reverence at sight.
The prison Tower of London, stain'd with crimes,
Recalls the tragedies of elder times.
Here fleets of vessels are launch'd into birth,
To circumnavigate the piecemeal earth,
And like a fortress gird our little isle
From foreign navies, and their landing foil.
The home of strangers, and workshop of art,
For manufactures famed, and warmth of heart;
Here the nest egg of industry is laid,
And competition stimulates our trade,
Where fashionable shops, and wares the best,
Attract the public to the far famed west;
Where gaiety and pleasure soothe the mind,
O'ertaxed with thought and business of mankind;
Where mansious, gardens, parks and lakes delight,
And various amusements all invite;
With royal palaces and works of fame,
By architects of genius, rank and name.
Where unique relics in museums lie,
With wrecks and sculptures of antiquity;

Choice libraries in colleges abound,—
In reading rooms, and classic spots of ground ;
With picture galleries and works of art,
Which interest and charm, or touch the heart.
Music and singing socially combine
To elevate the soul and taste refine.
To their suburban villas cits retire,
After the sunset of that globe of fire,
And in the season leave the busy hives,
For seaside breezes to prolong their lives.
Bards and composers to retreats retire,
Where the sublime and picturesque inspire,
And shun the noise and bustle of the town,
For groves of solitude to muse alone.
An isle of beauty where the blushing rose,
In the sweet face of lovely woman grows,
Whose beaming countenance with smiles is lit,
To cheer the festive circle with her wit ;
The helpmate and the counterpart of man,
Nature's desire, and Providence's plan.
The swarming population overgrown
Is scatter'd o'er the Earth and broadcast thrown :
Sprung from our loins to foreign climes they roam
In quest of fortune and a settled home.

SIR WALTER SCOTT.

The Wizard of the North, a blazing star
Of the first magnitude, attracts from far
All those who honour genius and renown,
To pay their homage to the 'Great Unknown'.
His country teems with heather, lochs, bald hills,
Which to behold with admiration fills,
As from Ben Nevis' snow-white lofty height
To huge Ben Lomond you extend your sight:
The dreary moor and solitary pass
In wild and rugged scenery surpass
The rich and fertile; while a foreign air
Is given to those who kilt and bonnet wear;
Looking so martial, picturesque and strange,
The costumed natives of the highland range.
Romance with legendary lore has flung
Their magic influence through the lays he sung;
He charms you with traditions, while he brings
His images before you as he sings.

His genius hovers round the Calton hill
Which shelters Holyrood, serene and still!
From which as by enchantment, marble white,
Springs modern Athens, lofty, noble, light!
    From this gay, populous, and fertile scene,
The panorama glides behind its screen,
Unfolding other objects to the view,
Of solitary grandeur passing through.
Hills beyond hills, and clustering mountains rise,
Grey, bald and heathery to the misty skies,
Which overhang the Teviots and the Tweed,
Where softer scenes the stern and grand succeed!
A pile of ruins in the midst appears,
Deserted skeletons ; and old in years,
A solitary spectre of the past,
In keeping with the dreary, wild, and vast.
The shade of Melrose, once so fair and bright,
In widow's weeds and sorrow, peers in sight,
Veiled in the deepest mourning, hollow eyed,
And yet majestic in her fallen pride.
Where are her satellites ? deluded slaves ?
And echo answers,—in their silent graves!
Here black-veiled nuns secured a safe retreat,
And holy fathers found their Paraclete,

From piety or disappointed love
The world exchanging for a heaven above.
Dead to the world, a human sacrifice,
A selfish and unnatural device,
Abhorrent to the instincts of mankind,
The laws of nature, and God's purposed mind !

    O'er these deserted ruins Time has thrown
Its dark and length'ning shadow ; stone on stone
Lies scatter'd in disorder round the pile,
The moss-grown fragments of the nave and aisle :
We pause upon its desolate remains,
Its grotesque griffins, monumental names,
And in abstracted reverie recall
Its strength and beauty, and inglorious fall.
The heart of Bruce, brought from the Holy Land,
Was here enshrin'd amidst a patriot band,
Who fought for glory in their country's cause,
Or lost their lives in feuds and border wars.
The soil is sacred, underneath its crust
Repose the good and great in hallow'd dust.

    There lingers round this old time-favoured spot
The venerable shade of Walter Scott,
Who threw a magic influence o'er the place :
We all around his sparkling genius trace.

By that same wand, and rising from the ground
As by enchantment, Abbotsford is found.
In the creations of his gifted mind,
Nobility of thought and dreams we find,
The fictions of romance ran through his veins
And winding nerves, to quick conceiving brains ;
In flights of fancy and inventive power,—
In local tales and legendary lore,—
In antiquarian records of the past,
His stores were inexhaustible and vast.
His images in old traditions rise,
Like picture galleries before our eyes,
Mingled with stirring incidents apart,
And moving scenes which touch the tender heart,
Throwing a wizard's spell around the whole,
O'erpowering into ecstasies the soul !
    Proud of our poets, many spots invite
To interest and gratify the sight ;
Familiar with their works we seek the place,
Which them inspired, and try those scenes to trace,
Which visions and imaginative power
Created in a contemplative hour ;
And lingering pause as if in hope to find
The glowing exhibitions of their mind.

Beyond this spot his costly mansion rose,
Sequester'd in plantations which enclose,
Surround and shelter underneath the hill,
Where all is cheerless, solitary, still !
A melancholy spectacle of woe,
Deserted in its pride ;—a house of show !
The classic seat of wealth and world-wide fame,
Th' abode of genius and an honour'd name,
Where kindred spirits and the Muses met
The great magician ere his sun-rays set !
Here were collected books and works of art,
With the companions dearest to his heart.
And antique armour hung his antler'd hall,
With relics, banners, fossils, urns, and all
That wealth commands and grandeur could desire,
To please, instruct, preserve what all admire.
When lo ! electric clouds appear in sight,
Charged with the venom of devouring blight,
Which settled on his fortunes none could save,
And brought his hairs with sorrow to the grave.
Like an eclipse, alas ! he pass'd away,
His soul emerging into realms of day.
O'er his remains at Dryburgh shed a tear,
And in your memory's tablet hold him dear.

NEWSTEAD ABBEY.

In Sherwood forest oaks and firs are spread,
And other sylvan monarchs rear their head;
These in the primitive old times ran wild,
Ere culture tamed Dame Nature's darling child;
When haughty barons with their neighbours warr'd,
And moated castles hostile entrance barr'd;
When knights and squires their feudal rights main-
    tain'd,
And petty warfare through the country reign'd.
Uncultivated woods exist no more;
Where rose the forest or the plain before,
Rich agricultural fields and golden corn
Adorn the teeming land where woods were born.
　　Conceal'd from view within the umbrageous wood,
With his freebooters, outlaw'd Robin Hood,
The terror of the country round, held sway,
And levied blackmail on the king's highway:

His feats of valour, daring enterprise,
Picturesque costume and abrupt surprise,
With generous instincts, and his self command,
Attach'd his followers, a faithful band ;—
An armed banditti, powerful in their day,
Surprised the equestrian traveller on his way,
In tangled woods and forests as he rode
Upon the beaten track without a road ;
Or on the heath waylaid at fall of night,
When all was dark and lonesome without light ;
And the shrill whistle summon'd to their aid
The outpost scouts and those in ambuscade,
Who seem'd to spring like genii from the ground,
With a command to ' halt' as they surround.
' Stand and deliver', follow'd by a blow,
Showed the stern nature of the hostile foe ;
And wait the pleasure of the gallant chief,
Who on all travellers exacts a fief
For passing through his manor and domains,
Where the highwayman in his lair remains.
The fine is fix'd and paid ; ere they depart
The chivalrous captain shows a generous heart,
Appoints an escort to convoy them through
The devious track, and bids his guests adieu ;

But if refractory found, they're prisoners made,
And kept in durance till their ransom's paid.
To gentle ladies he was all-polite,
As any courtier, gentleman, or knight,
And with the priesthood under his control
Shared the wild game, to save his guilty soul.

Within th' entangled forest's bush retreat,
The gothic pile of Newstead found its seat;
Where once the abbey's bell was heard to ring,
And the veil'd sisters evening vespers sing;
The brides of heaven with consecrated vows,
And solemn service their great Head espouse;
Retired from strife, the world, temptation, sin,
The holy family dwells a heaven within,
A house of piety, of prayer, and praise,
To purify, exalt, refine, and raise
The soul to its Creator, and aspire
To loftier objects, and to regions higher.

These skeleton remains and Gothic hall
Depress the spirits and the heart appal,
Presenting us with glimpses of the past,
O'er which the tide of memory, ebbing fast,
Restores and fills the mind with what would seem
The fading image of a passing dream.

The stately pile, the castellated tower,
And storied chapel, in a fatal hour
Suppress'd with other monasteries, decay'd,
Razed, pillaged, stripped, they long neglected laid:
Out of their ashes, and curtail'd in size,
We see a motley modern structure rise;—
A lordly mansion, a baronial seat,
A rich ancestral family retreat;
Whose lofty pannel'd roof and oaken floor,
Quadrangular cloisters and groin'd corridor,
Attest the former use and antique style
Of this once sacred venerable pile;
Whose solemn echoes trembling fears impart,
As they come thrilling through the nervous heart.
Fantastic forms and shadows fill the trees,
And hollow voices load the whispering breeze:
Strange noises, cracking doors, unearthly sounds,
From vaulted roof or subterranean grounds:
Romantic scenes and figures flit before,
Like magical illusions, and restore
The legendary fictions of an age,
With superstition stamp'd upon its page,
When memory and tradition handed down
The myths, and fabled stories of renown.

In these monastic ruins we may trace
The ancestry of Byron's noble race,
Who with the Norman conqueror came o'er,
And vanquish'd Harold on Britannia's shore.
Their offspring was of melancholy mood,
And saw no laurels in his birth or blood,
But felt the spirit's influence to flow
Within him, oft-times kindle to a glow
Of inspiration in his musing mind.
A flash of light rush'd swifter than the wind
When dreams of fancy to his sight appear
Transparent beings of some heavenly sphere,
Or the Elysian fields come crowding round,
With sylph-like nymphs whose voices softly sound.
  The Abbey had been long his father's home,
But he to foreign lands was giv'n to roam,
And dwelt but briefly at th' ancestral seat,
A lonely, long neglected, dull retreat,
Whence old time monuments are scatter'd round,
With traces of what once was hallow'd ground;
With sylvan deities of cloven feet,
And horned heads in masquerade you meet;
While gardens geometrical in style,
And shady walks with ferneries beguile.

His misanthropic spirit haunts the place,
And every shadow brings him face to face:
He flits before you in the playful breeze,
You hear his music in the whispering trees;—
In echoes of your footfall on the ground,
And answering voices from the hills around.

You lingering pause with mute inquiring gaze,
And in a reverie call up bygone days,
And fancy, as you taste the bubbling spring,
You see the monks, and hear the virgins sing.
But the cold earth their withering bones contains;
It is the poet who supremely reigns,
And draws the pilgrim from his natal shore,
The early fate of Byron to deplore:
He views with interest curious relics there,
And sees his inspirations everywhere;—
In yonder oak he planted with his hand,
And 'Boatswain's' monument sarcastic plann'd,
Th' initial letters cut out of the tree,—
The winding walks fill'd with his minstrelsy,—
Th' arcadian groves which listen'd to his Muse,—
The lake whose mazy winds and banks you lose,—
The hanging woodlands with the pastoral sound,
And Claude-like pictures in the landscape found,

The still retreat with its secluded calm,
The poet's birthplace and its secret charm.
All that was mortal Hucknall church contains,
For there repose ' Childe Harold's' cold remains ;
In the same vault where those he sprang from sleep,
But over him the pilgrim comes to weep.
His darling Ada, once his hope and pride,
Now lies by her distinguished father's side :
A mural monument records their fate,
The closing fate of all, though blank the date !

———————

KIRKE WHITE.

Lock'd in his closet by the dim lamp's light,
He mused away the vigil hours of night,
Knitting his eyebrows with inflated vein,
As if conception overstrain'd his brain:
Absent in mind and swallow'd up in thought,
With little learning Kirke White was self-taught;
Till Cambridge welcomed him and open threw
The closed up portals to his longing view.
In these square cloisters and scholastic walls,
Rise Gothic towers, churchspires, and ancient halls,
Which in the distance fascinate the eye,
And look majestic beacons of the sky;
Encircled with green pastures,—gardens wide,
Huge forest trees and Cam's o'erflowing tide,
With private avenue, Arcadian walk,
Inviting to retirement or to talk.
  The venerable shadows of the past,
Throughout these grey and lichen'd walls are cast;

The rich stained glass, groin'd roof, and carved stalls,
Preserved in these old colleges and halls,
With portraits of the founders who endow'd,
And majesty who patronage bestow'd,
With learned fellows,—lights of other days,
Inflate our admiration and our praise.
Enrich'd with books and manuscripts unroll'd,
In musty papyrus and parchments old,
With marble busts and statues of the great,
Museum collections of a mythic date,
With storied windows from the sacred page,
Stain'd glass and paintings of the middle age.
The youthful minstrel feels a prompting swell,
And his lyre joins with those who sing so well;
His infant melodies in lyrics burst,
And at the Muses' fount he slakes his thirst
In mournful idyls, odes, and songs of love,
While basking in the shades of Clifton grove,
A still retreat for meditative minds,
Which the Trent laves as gracefully it winds,
And where the lowing kine by instinct led,
In slow procession reach its shallow bed,
To taste its nectar and to cool their feet,
And moderate the summer's scorching heat.

Then recreate in pastures richly green:
'Tis nature's picture and a pastoral scene.
Across the flood what cheering landscapes rise,
To gratify the sight and tranquillize
The weary soul by worldly cares oppress'd,
And give it that sweet solace, mental rest!
While the all-rapturous lark on soaring wings,
In summer's dazzling sunshine quavering sings,
And the whole grove of songsters load the breeze,
With vocal music in the nodding trees.

 The youths in their collegiate cap and gown,
Give animation to the quiet town;
The spacious garden walks are all alive,
Like bees that cluster round the swarming hive:
So these industrious Attic bees their store
Of classic learning swarm at wisdom's door.
Contemplative amid the busy throng,
Harvesting knowledge and the sweets of song,
The youthful White, in labours too severe,
O'ertask'd his brain and lies a martyr here.
The love of letters and desire of fame,
With a position piety might claim,
Were his ambition and his earthly aim.
His early fate and studious life impart
A moral lesson to the kindred heart,

Where sympathy's moist eye and heaving breast,
Through which the gentler passions are express'd,
A softening influence lend to that pale face
Serenely mild, whose genius here we trace.
Alas! how many toil and undermine
A sickly constitution, then decline!

PARIS.

The model city with attractions blazed,
And to the full the lingering stranger gazed
With admiration! Fashion, taste, display,
Decoy the rambling traveller on his way:
Silks, jewels, tapestry adorn the shops,
With glitttering mirrors where the lounger stops;
Dress, fashion, gaiety, and pompous show
Dazzle, amuse, pursue where'er you go;
The café, restaurant, theatre, ball,
Emblem their life and character withal;
Fill'd with the pleasure-seeking, worldly, gay,
Paris is France epitomized they say.
Of tasteful genius, volatile, polite,
The people are light-hearted, fickle, bright.
The pure soft atmosphere, and clear blue sky
Exhilarate, and brighten up the eye;
These animate the spirits,—cheer the sight,
Infuse a glowing warmth and give delight:

And here, attracted by its world-wide fame,
Assembled meet the proud and great of name :
The busy hives of industry thrive here,
And politics and literature appear.
Triumphal arches of elaborate art
Excite your admiration, and impart
Surprise and wonder to the ravish'd sight,
So beautifully wrought and exquisite.
In classic forms the graceful figures rise
From marble fountains of colossal size,
With nymphs and mermaids sporting in the stream,
In mythic characters of what they seem ;
Equestrian statues with symbolic sign,
And monuments past memories enshrine ;
With choicest flowers of aromatic scent,
Where boulevard avenues their shelter lent
From the meridian heat, and which at night
Blaze up in jets of artificial light.
On either shore, the river proudly flows,
And noble palaces and columns rose :
The Tuileries, Hotel de Ville, St. Cloud,
The Palais Royal, Notre Dame, and Rue,
With Champs Elysées and the Bois Boulogne,
Attract the gay and pleasure-seeking throng ;

With the Louvre's treasures brought from every shore,
And venerable works of days of yore;
With classic fragments sleeping side by side,
Of extinct nations scatter'd far and wide.
The costly decorated churches stand,
Memorials to the pious of the land,
Whose lofty columns of antique design,
With illustrations, stamp them half divine.
Outside the city walls repose the dead,
In Père La Chaise with monuments o'erspread,
From whose allhallow'd fane, exalted height,
The imperial capital's reveal'd to sight.

He in the Louvre amongst the works of art
Most pleasure found, and gave up half his heart;
For there in unison with all he felt,
He mused o'er works which raise as well as melt,
The god-like sympathies of human kind,
Exalting the nobility of mind.
Here painting, sculpture, and remains combine
To cultivate, enlighten, and refine
The manners and the customs of our age,
Exhibited upon the public stage
Of private history, in grand review,
Pictorial of the fabulous or true,

With the remains of nations proud and great,
Who long succumb'd to fortune and to fate.

At Champs Elysées youth and age look gay,
Let out upon a sunshine holiday,
And fond of pleasure as they are of play :
All joyous, sprightly, happy, blithe, and free,
A wealthy, fashionable company,
Assembled from all nations of the earth,
For leisure and amusement, health and mirth ;
Who promenade around th' orchestral band,
And join the fairest daughters of the land,
Who sit in groups with needle-work in hand.

SWITZERLAND.

From the voluptuous capital of France,
Through which in passing we but caught a glance,
We like a bird of passage swiftly fly
To Alpine regions and vermilion sky,
To tour the country round and sight expand,
With the romantic scenes of Switzerland;
By route of Brussels, for a bird's-eye view
Of the red battle-field of Waterloo!
Where on the monumental mound a tear,
Will start for those brave warriors sleeping here!
From thence across by diligence and rail,
We enter the cantons by mouth of Basle;
A key to the dominions of the hills,
A prospect which with admiration fills!
    Where lofty scenery elevates the mind,
We soar beyond the Earth new worlds to find,
And guage the broad infinity of space,
Its systems, comets, suns and stars to trace;

E'en so the hills ambitiously we climb
To view the grand, majestic, and sublime;
And scale the rocks with alpine-stock and feet,
Where heaven and earth in social council meet,
To plant our flag upon the giddy height
Of misty Righi bursting into sight!
  At sunset where the tints begin to fade,
And twilight lingers into deep'ning shade,
We leave the infant village as we rise,
Tier upon tier, launched into other skies.
With gasping breath we pause, and turn to look
On distant objects and the route we took,
Watching with eager gaze the close of day,
Which slowly dwindles ere it melts away,
Then sinks into th' horizon's changing views
In all the colours of the rainbow's hues;
When out of darkness springs the queen of night,
As sentinel till morning's blush of light!
Then to our task return, ascend this hill,
And then another, and a higher still.
The mountaineer attempts the dangerous pass,
And often disappears down the crevasse,
Which lies concealed beneath the treacherous snow,
And whirls him into gorges deep below.

Where snowy fields surround the mountain's breast,
In a rude hut we midway take our rest
At nightfall, when the crescent moon shines clear,
And heaven's blue vault lies open everywhere.
Before the mists of night begin to break,
Or light seen struggling through the eastern gate,
Restless we rise our object to pursue,
At early dawn our journey to renew.
The meteoric showers incessant fly
From east to west across the spangled sky:
The Kulm is veil'd in the encircling mist,
With the three lakes encompass'd in the midst,
Until the bugle or the Alpine horn
At the first blush of day awakes the morn.
The mountain tips develope as we rise,
Increase in number, and expand in size:
The morning star shines like an orb of gold,
The dewy atmosphere is Arctic cold;
Succeeded by a flash of sparkling light,
When suddenly the sun leaps into sight;
Kindling the eastern range of hills afar,
When it extinguish'd every fading star,
And lit with rosy pink the changing sky,
Which flash'd like lightning into flames on high.

Unearthly grandeur blazed on all around,
As up the steep we climbed and summit crown'd,
A glorious panorama to survey,
Which stretch'd to Bernese Oberland away,
O'er mountain ridges, lakes, and vallies green,
With clustering groups of gilded hills between;
Enthroned and mantled in a robe of snow,
In contrast to the roseate hues below;
Mid purple skies and streaks of amber light,
As if a new creation rose in sight.
Absorb'd in contemplation and struck mute,
We stood like statues which had taken root.
The hungry eyes enraptured at the sight,
Glow at the feast with increased appetite,
And in a pleasing reverie we deem
The painted landscape a pictorial dream!
Lakes, forests, hills assembled at our feet,
In one vast prospect all united meet.
As if by magical illusion seen,
A flowery paradise, a fairy scene!
Here scatter'd chalets glitter'd in the sun,
And hunted chamois through the woodlands run,
While seas of mist hung on the mountain's brow,
And shut from sight the living world below:

The cromlech altars scatter'd o'er the plains,
Look like some rude druidical remains.

   Before us is the Jungfrau midway seen,
Sublime and grand with its terrific scene;
The mountain seem'd in labour, and upheav'd,
As if to bring forth what it had conceived:
An avalanche of snow came bounding o'er,
And petrified us with its thundering roar,
O'erwhelming in its rapid headlong fall
The sloping valley and the glacier wall;
Resembling ice-fields coated o'er with snow,
Congeal'd and melted with the drifting floe.
The savage grandeur of the Devil's bridge,
Suspended in the air on Titlis ridge,
Now menaces with its dark shaggy frown,
To hem us in, and in its torrents drown,
As they came rolling through with deaf'ning roar,
Filling the loose-strung nerves with shuddering o'er.
The foaming waterfalls and wild cascades
Leap down the dreadful precipice to shades
Where sunken rocks, in reservoirs below,
In streams divide the mountain's overflow;
Whose crystal showers of spray from rocks rebound,
And howling thunders echo all around;

The silvery fountains, sparkling in the sun,
Are by reflection into rainbows spun.

From various points of view the fairy Rhine,
Gracefully flowing, clear and serpentine,
Looks out amongst the clustering hills which rise,
With schlosses crown'd that pierce the leaden skies.
Fir forests with dark foliage of green,
Darken the air and close up all the scene;
The verdant lawns and meadows at your feet,
With avenues afford a snug retreat;
Luxuriant orchards full of promise bloom,
And fine magnolias yield their rich perfume,
Where vine-clad terraces on either side,
And floating bridges cross the mazy tide :
Here legends and traditions, myths and rhymes,
Recall the crusades of heroic times.

By Zermatt route Monte Rosa we ascend,
And on experienced trusty guides depend,
Who up the perpendicular hew steps,
And fearless clamber like expert adepts ;
Above the eyrie of the eagle's flight,
Or grazing deer who timidly take fright,
The cracking glaciers roll their thunder down
The craggy ridges with a piercing groan ;

R

As when the Earth convulsed in pieces flew,
And in one seething cauldron chaos threw.
The snow accumulates in clefts and rocks,
The growth of ages, into solid blocks,
Which melt in pouring streams before the sun,
But freeze again before his course is run.
The icy glacier's arms stretch far and wide,
And like a rolling river oft divide.
This beetling cliff pass'd by and narrow pass,
Lie scenes of many a tragedy, alas!
The adventurer, in trying a glissade,
Oft comes to grief and in the convent's laid;
The morgue at the hospice, touching sight!
Will thaw the feelings and the soul affright.
Yon cairn and cross a monument supply
To some lost friend enshrin'd in memory.

Descending from this height where all look'd dead,
You face the south and find the winter fled;
The Alpine peaks and glaciers fade from view,
The climate changes, and a sky of blue
Adorns the landscape, calm, serene, and bright,
Where Italy unveils herself to sight,
In all her winning charms and gay attire,
Whose loveliness and beauty all admire.

The placid lakes like glorious mirrors shine,
And round the mountain gracefully entwine;
The coy retreating brook and shrubbery glade
Afford a grateful and refreshing shade
From summer heat, while in the dirty town
Miasma blights with its grim threat'ning frown!
  In our excursions shifting scenes arise,
Where danger lurks to mar our enterprize;
The sunbright sky with clouds is split in twain,
And in a moment drenches you with rain;
The treacherous climate without warning given,
Opens upon you the floodgates of heaven.
We suddenly discern the Matterhorn,
Of giant pedigree, aërial born!
Imperial monarch of a noble line,
Allied to the majestic and divine!
In solitary grandeur it appears
Enthroned in pendent icicles of years!
Clothed with the sombre pines or chestnut trees,
Whose lofty plumes are waving in the breeze.
Ferns, scarlet rhododendrons, rich and bright,
And Alpine flowers of every hue invite;
Mid rushing waterfalls and rivers deep,
Whose headlong torrents down the chasm leap,

As the Niagara with artillery roar,
Reverberates around from shore to shore.
Here rustic bridges cross the angry flood,
And patient anglers watch with line and rod.
A spectral fog-bow like a sign appears,
And haunts the mind with preternatural fears;
Like to an apparition in a dream,
So mythical and shadowy did it seem!

Chamounix now presents itself to sight,
In all the splendour of the rays of light,
With mountain scenery and the Mer de Glace,
The Grands Mulets and lofty wall'd up pass,
Whose snow-white peaks in tiers of clouds are lost,
Inlaid with glaciers and perpetual frost,
And frigid as the pole with ice and snow,
He wears a diadem upon his brow.
As unconnected with the things of Time,
He regal looks in this impressive clime,
Still, stern, and solemn!—ruins of the past,
On which you ruminate and stand aghast!
Winter and summer here alternate reign,
Amidst the lofty, broken, Alpine chain;
The snow-clad mountains in their fleecy vest
And broider'd robes of purity are dress'd.

Amidst the nether range encircling rise
The sturdy monarchs of inferior size ;
The Aiguilles stand out in bold relief,
As if in adoration of their chief.
The grand and beautiful are here combin'd,
And fill with wonder the astonish'd mind :
Its rich and verdant valley lies beneath,
And enclosed pastures form a flowery wreath,
Where the whole landscape stretches out its arms
In nymph-like fashion to display its charms.
The voice of eloquence has found a tongue,
The hymn of praise has not been left unsung ;
But where's the fancy ?   Where the painter's art,
The landscape's faithful image to impart ?

The milch goats feed upon the mountain's side,
As on you travel with your mule and guide.
Turning a Coll, Mont Blanc appears in view,
And from the valley our fix'd gaze withdrew,
To feast upon the pinnacles of snow,
Reflected in the silvery lake below.
Here various peeps and panoramic views
Before you glide, as riveted you muse
Upon some great convulsion of the earth,
Which split asunder when launch'd into birth ;

Or drowning flood, or at Creation's dawn,
Ere light was shed on that illumin'd morn ;
Or brutes foreshadow'd pre-historic man,
When after chaos order's laws began,
In preparation for the human race,
Who met in Eden with a fond embrace.

    While gathering clouds below invest the night,
The hills above still flame with lingering light,
Upon th' horizon till extinguish'd quite.
When Cynthia from her watch-tower in the sky
Lit up the jewell'd firmament on high.
The frozen glaciers coated o'er with snow,
By one false step precipitate below ;
Your balance lost, the slippery slope you slide,
And tied together, drag your trusty guide,
O'er the sharp edge from cliff to cliff you leap,
Into the gulf a thousand fathoms deep !
With broken limbs unconsciously you lie
A bleeding corpse of frail mortality !

    Crossing the Simplon, desolate and wild,
At dusk in winter when serene and mild,
The fickle weather changed, the wind blew cold,
And chill'd the spirits of both young and old.
The tourmentes cut through the thick-veil'd face,
Until the road we could no longer trace ;

The showers of hailstones and the flakes of snow
Clogg'd up the wheels, which could no further go ;
Horses stopp'd short half blinded with the gale,
When indistinctly we heard voices hail,
Which from the refuge came to help and save
From Death's cold touch the frozen out and brave !
And to the hospice of St. Bernard guide,
Through dangers that beset on every side ;
Met by the faithful dogs of purest breed,
Whose keen scent track'd and proved our friends in
    need.
To deeds of mercy train'd, they climb'd the height,
And reach the monastery by fall of night,
Receiv'd and welcomed by the worthy friars,
Who cheer'd with viands and log-blazing fires.
   As we to striking scenes our footsteps bend,
And from the valley to the hills ascend,
To breathe a purer atmosphere above,
Whose solemn grandeur all our feelings move ;
So on descending to the fertile vale,
Teeming with life we welcome with 'all hail'.
Smiling in beauty, cheerful to the sight,
The village and the picturesque delight.
Geneva ! rises with its towers and spires,
And crowded villas, and to rank aspires,

And with the rapid Rhone and violet lake,
Fringed round with trees upon your vision break :
Tame in comparison with the background
Of snow-clad mountains circling you around,
Whose rural pastures with the herdsman's bell,
And fertile hillocks gently slope and swell,
With wooded landscapes and pictorial views,
And simple wild flowers of the rainbow's hues.
The thrush and lark the gamut teach their young,
And fill the woods with their melodious song,
The finch and robin all in chorus sing,
And with the blackbird herald in the Spring.
The peasants in their picturesque attire,
And artless manners you must needs admire ;
But chief of beauties, lovely in a calm,
The glassy lake bewitches with a charm,
Where gentle zephyrs softly lull to rest,
Its piteous sighs and agitated breast :
Yon Castle* with its dreary prison walls,
Darken'd with death, the stoutest heart appals,
The torture chambers, rack, and thumbscrew press,
Drove innocent and guilty to confess,
And point to those inquisitorial crimes,
When barbarous feuds stained those blood-red times.

* Chillon.

In close proximity Lausanne, in fame
Basks in the sunshine of a classic name ;
Here sage philosophers of great renown,
Fled from their country and the Babel town,
To spend the evening of their lives apart,
Amid the objects dearest to their heart :
Here bards in rapture warbled forth their praise,
And glorified its beauties in their lays ;
Here spiral towers and monuments arise,
And nature's lovely pictures harmonize.
Seclusion in the suburbs may be found,
And pleasure yachts and sailing skiffs abound,
Mingled with music wafted o'er the lake,
Where all its sweet enchantments on you break.

ROME.

Enclosed in its seven hills the City lay,
In sad and mournful picturesque decay,
Rome and its Cæsars underneath repose,
And sepulchres their hallow'd dust enclose.
The mouldering remains and rampart wall
Are wrecks of time, and nodding to their fall.
Where temples, public baths, theatres stood,
Are silent deserts,—dreary solitude!
The great and fallen city we explore,
And in our swelling hearts her fate deplore.
Imperial edifices disinterr'd
Reveal the grandeur of which all have heard;
The pillar'd monuments of bronze or stone,
Are now with fruitful vineyards overgrown.
The wealthy Capitol in ruins laid,—
The Pantheon with vein'd marble all inlaid,—
The Colosseum of gigantic size,—
And broken columns, which like spectres rise,—

With Cæsar's Palace, and the catacombs,
And prostate Forums in their silent tombs.
The Arch Triumphal, with its public show,
Has disappear'd with bridge and portico :
The Arch of Titus and the Appian way
Invite the weary traveller to stay ;
The marble palaces and Palatine,
To dreamy musings on the past incline :
Abstracted, taciturn, you fix your gaze
On subterranean spoils of other days ;—
The Circus with its ostentatious shows,
And dens of wild beasts for the captive foes ;
The Basilica or old judgment hall,
With towers defaced, and crumbling lichen wall,
The colour'd marbles and mosaic floor,
Are specimens of art in days of yore ;
The dried up fountains which old Rome supplied,
And luxuries which puff'd her up with pride :
The Senate House which listen'd in debate
To orators of rank lies desolate,
The sculptured monuments and works of art
Display their faded beauty, and impart
A touching sadness to the human heart ;
And subterranean chambers shed a gloom,
Over the prostrate city in the tomb.

With sacrificial altars, hallow'd dust,
And casque and sword all coated o'er with rust,
Chains, armlets, rings, and ornaments of show,
Which add a beauty to the maiden's brow,
Preserv'd with sanctity and pious care,
In sad remembrance of what once they were.

The lawless Goths and Vandals from afar
Invaded Rome where raged intestine war,
And burnt th' Eternal City to the ground,
And pillaged and destroy'd the country round!

O'er these deserted remnants Time has spread
The blight of ages ; moss and weeds have fed
Like parasites upon their natural prey,
Where all the world is emblem'd by decay,
Belonging to the venerable past ;
And o'er the mind a pensive gloom is cast :
So much of *débris* ruins underlie,
Old, worn, and musty, that you pass them by ;
Romance and history round their memories cling ;
Their ancient fame and glory poets sing.
These mouldering relics crusted o'er with age,
Excite your interest and your thoughts engage,
With shelf-cramm'd archives of collected stores,
Bronze rusty urns, and coins from Tiber's shores,

Museums, exhibitions, gems of art,
With spectral ruins stare from every part,
The fragments of a city once so rife
With bristling arms and animated life !

    In contrast to these wrecks of elder days,
A modern structure now solicits praise,
Whose pinnacles and lofty dome arise,
In elevated grandeur to the skies.
Aërial amidst the stars sublime,
St. Peter's stands the wonder of our time ;
The Palace of the Vatican is there,
With its art specimens and treasures rare ;
Choice paintings, fountains, arms, and books adorn,
And ancient vestiges in fragments torn,
With marble statues of the good and great,
And sculptured monuments without a date.

251

POMPEII.

From Rome to Pompeii our footsteps tread,
To crush the ashes of the prostrate dead.
Entomb'd alive, the city underground,
After the lapse of centuries is found
(Sponged from the map and hidden from the eye,
But known to fame and immortality)
Beneath a stratum which had buried deep,
The living multitude while in their sleep.
The rumbling thunders of Vesuvius burst,
And vomited forth pumice, fire and dust!
From the rent fissures showers of stones descend,
And sheets of flame an awful interest lend ;
Fresh fuel open'd wide its hungry jaws,
And then relaxed into a solemn pause,
The dreary night was midway on its course,
The air was darken'd and the winds grew hoarse,
When subterranean thunders shook the earth,
Seized with the labour pains of giving birth.

From the volcanic mountain's awful brow,
Down which the fiery rivers roll'd below,
The tossing mountain like an earthquake rose,
And the Earth filled with agonising throes ;
The sable clouds from out its nostrils rise,
O'erspread the mouths and canopied the skies ;
The fire descends like rain,—the lava pours
Down the hill's sides in torrents and loud roars :
From out its cones the crackling entrails fly,
In hissing showers across the smoke-fill'd sky.
The bellowing artillery confin'd,
Burst from their fetters to the raging wind,
Like an explosion from the cannon's mouth ;
Terrific grandeur reigns from north to south.

The previous night they had retired to rest,
And parents bless'd their children and caress'd,
Not doubting that to-morrow's sun would rise
And animate with light the drowsy skies :
Engagements, business, pleasure and renown,
Would be all rife as usual in the town.

All was confusion in the public street,
Each flying to some sheltering retreat,
Bewilder'd, terrified, in mute despair,
They rush half naked through the sultry air,

Intent upon their lives and wealth to save,
The fugitives went forth to find a grave:
Choked with the suffocating clouds of smoke,
Through which the lightning's vivid flashes broke;
And throngs of human beings thread their way
Towards the sea-shore where some shipping lay;
As if from life to death the mass were hurl'd
Into the vortex of the spectral world.
The shrieks of children frighten and appal,
And frantic women to their husbands call;
With agonising groans they rend the air,
And lift their hands to Heaven in wild despair,
With the last gasp of life, and breathe a prayer!

All was deserted, desolate and dark,
Save here a flambeau,—there a flying spark,
Fear seized on all the panic-stricken crowd,
And all bewail'd Pompeii's fate aloud.
Sparks burst in flames,—the conflagration spread
From house to house, and on their treasures fed.

Some grope within their homes to find the door,
To see the blaze, and hear the clamorous roar.
Wildly they ran about from room to room,
To find an exit, or to meet their doom.
Ashes and fire descend, and stifling smoke
Enter their dwellings, and the inmates choke;

The sultry atmosphere gains on their strength,
And one by one lies prostrate at his length;
For refuge some then to the cellars fly,
To eke out life, and starve, and shortly die:
Struck dumb they look'd aghast with dread and fear,
Without a friend or ray of hope to cheer;
In deep anxiety some spend the night,
And watch the slow return of morning light;
Their destiny was seal'd, their struggling breath
Collapsed within the sepulchre of death;
Frantic with fear and madness men despair,
And grope in darkness, or by th' flickering glare
Of the night lamp, they shriek and shout aloud,
For help beneath th' impenetrable cloud:
As in a chamber'd mine, in suites of rooms,
Some died a lingering death in stately tombs.
After two thousand years have pass'd away,
These tombs were opened, and their relics lay
Around the hearth, or huddled side by side,
Near to the torch-lamp where they slept and died!
Exposed to public view, unroof'd and bare,
You see their furniture and earthenware,
With the remains of fuel, wine, and bread,
And all their household pets, but all were dead!

S

Their jewels, statues, coins, urns, vases, rings,
Bronze ornaments, and baths, and curious things,
O'er which old Time his darkening shadow flings!
   No record tells their sufferings, misery, woe,
Buried alive in villas deep below;
Above their ashes, dust and scoria rise;
As in a trance, the sleeping city lies
In solemn silence, prostrate in the dust,
Lost and entomb'd beneath a solid crust.
The enceinte city, like a child unborn,
Enclosed from view was buried in and gone,
With all the public buildings great and small,
Theatre, forum, market-place and all!

THE RHINE.

From Pompeii the traveller takes his flight
To more congenial climes which charm the sight.
Enchanting and soul-soothing lovely Rhine !
Whose terraced banks are trellised with the vine,
Whose creeping tendrils up the summit climb,
Encircled with a chain of hills sublime
And beautiful ! tiers beyond tiers emerge ;
As we ascend, its graceful banks diverge,
And as the river winds and circles through,
Present a panorama to the view,
With ever varying pictures that disclose
The fertile valley, and the sweet repose
Of pastoral life, in its secluded nooks,
With mountain torrents and their silver brooks.
Cologne's cathedral with its Gothic spires
And architectural ornaments inspires :
Its fragrant waters yield a rich perfume,
Revive the fainting,—scent the crowded room.

Baronial castles on their hilly height,
In regal grandeur open to the sight;
Deserted ruins, crumbling in decay,
Speak of past glory and a feudal day,
When martial deeds and chivalrous renown
Stirr'd chiefs and barons to dispute a crown.
Between the verdant slopes the village spire
Stands in the foreground, and the hills retire;
Large rafts of timber down the river glide,
Delightful chateaus rise on either side.
The Drachenfels are rich in towering wood,
And mantling forests crown the brotherhood;
Where many a legendary tale of old,
After the lapse of centuries is told;
Romance has its poetic fiction strung,
And druid priests and bards their idyls sung,
Investing every place with mythic lore,
And famed divinities, and sprites of yore.
The Andernach burst suddenly in view,
Behind a narrow pass with its tableaux,
Unfolding figured landscapes to the sight,
Smiling in beauty, calm, serene, and bright.
Enclosing mountains stretch from side to side,
And seem to bar both vessel and the tide,

But on approaching, open and divide!
The barrier past, you turn to look behind,
And changing scenes and newer beauties find.
Near the Moselle, are forts upon the shore,
Coblentz and Ehrenbreitstein rise before,
Join'd with a bridge of boats which spans the Rhine,
So playful, picturesque, and serpentine ;
Dotted with islands of romantic fame,
Which gave them a traditionary name.
Through these Arcadian nooks and still retreats,
Encamp no armies,—pass no hostile fleets.
Retired from life, to which it bids adieu,
The modest convent often peers in view ;
Luxuriant pastures, slopes, and verdant dale,
As they ascend before us seem to sail ;
The soaring lark, lost in the soft blue sky,
Enraptures with aërial minstrelsy.
The kine repose in pastures rich and green,
And all around looks like a fairy scene.
Mysterious echoes fly from hill to hill,
And timid minds with superstition fill :
We thread the currents, landscapes rich and clear
Encircle us on all sides, and appear
Like the creations of a poet's mind,
Or gems of art by Nature's hand design'd !

Claude's, Wilson's, Turner's lovely pictures rise,
Touch'd by the magic wand before your eyes.
With flowers of every hue the garden smiles,
Whose glowing warmth of colouring beguiles.
Fine aromatic odours fill the gale,
And the sweet breath of summer all inhale.
In calm seclusion far from noise and strife,
The rural peasant leads a happy life,
Free from exciting scenes, ambition, care,
Which the inhabitants of cities share.
The hills diminish, Bieberich and Mayence
Dissolve the views which fade into romance!

BADEN SCHLOSS.

At Baden Schloss, which now in ruin lies
Upon the hill where nature's landscapes rise,
Imagine a deep cavern by the side
Of the twin Schloss, with mouth all opening wide!
Dark, dismal, and suspicious to the sight,
A gloomy vault without a ray of light.
Trembling with fear you enter first and pause,
Remembering the inquisitorial laws.
A cicerone with torchlight soon appears
To guide you through and mitigate your fears.
With cautious steps and slow as you descend,
The winding labyrinth seems to have no end :
The daylight's faded which you left behind,
And ill forebodings seize upon your mind :
Nocturnal darkness environs around,
And hollow footsteps echo from the ground.
The dungeon doors are solid slabs of stone,
Which ope on rusty pivots with a groan,
As through the subterranean arch you go
To a stone chamber in th' abyss below.

Damp, cold, and cobwebb'd, with a secret way,
That closes up the cheerful light of day;
Where monsters in the shape of men preside,
Styled 'Inquisition', who the prisoners tried.
As into the infernal realms you come,
You think of racks, rings, thumbscrews, and are
    dumb;
And fancy Satan with his hell-born crew
In judgment sitting upon men they knew,
Who knew not them! blindfolded were the eyes,
Of all their victims, chain'd and in disguise.
Condemn'd to torture by the demons there,
For private pique, or faith, or lands they share.
Near this a figure of the Virgin stood,
With outstretch'd arms and thirsting for their blood;
As they were forced to kiss th' enamelled face,
And she mechanically to embrace;
Which touch'd a secret spring (forged deep in hell)
When through a trap-door down the victims fell
Into the dark deep dungeon of a well.
Fancy the echo through the shaft resound,
In rolling volumes underneath the ground,
Where knives and spikes on wheels were thickly sewn,
Impaled alive and wrung th' expiring groan.

EPITAPHS.

I.

What deep emotions in the bosom rise,
What sorrow from the heart springs to the eyes,
When the world closes on the friends we love,
And their enfranchised souls escape above!
Still more the melting eye and heart deplore,
A mother,—when that mother is no more!
Who watch'd o'er infancy's unconscious hours,
And strew'd o'er childhood's path the choicest flowers,
Under the shadow of whose wings we grew,
Shelter'd from every ill that near us drew,
Who bless'd us with her love through life's rough road,
And dying left us to the care of God!

II.

The stream of time hath borne her to the tomb,
   And veil'd her time-worn relics from our eyes!
But memory's lamp will cheer our pensive gloom,
   And light us to her dwelling in the skies!

III.

Immortalized in memory's sacred shrine,
　And mourn'd by those in life she held most dear,
There needs no flattering ostentatious line,
　To tell the worth and goodness buried here!

IV.

Her pilgrimage of life is o'er,—
Her sun is set!—she groans no more!
Death o'er her path his shadow threw,
Long ere she bade the world adieu:
Severe affliction seal'd her doom,
And long prepared her for the tomb!

V.

　Sever'd from her he held most dear,
　　While travelling life's rough road;
　How oft his footsteps linger'd here,
　　To ease his mental load!

　Time pluck'd the rooted sting of grief,
　　And sooth'd his suffering mind:
　He felt his pilgrimage was brief,
　　While struggling on behind.

A glimmering twilight settled round
    The evening of his days,
When he some consolation found
    In pious prayer and praise.

VI.

If virtues and benevolence of heart,
    With genial manners our best friends endear,
What can express our feelings when we part,
    Or speak our sorrow like a silent tear ?
Our only solace, 'twixt regret and love,
Is—they are happier in the realms above !

VII.

Affection's tribute we to memory pour,
And grieve to think our dear ones are no more.
The spark of life which kindled in his eye,
Has vanish'd to ethereal realms on high.
So fade the flowers,—so leaves of autumn fall,—
Our spirits to depress, and mind appal.
A dreary winter to our loss succeeds,
Our soul is rayless, and our lone heart bleeds ;

Our home is desolate,—a withering gloom
Hangs o'er each thought reflected from the tomb,
Which we revisit with a mournful sigh,
With some foreboding we must shortly die.

269

MONODY.

THE dulcet strains of music fill the ear,
Though silent is the voice of vocal power,
That charm'd with ecstasy the list'ning throng
Who hung on her aërial echoing notes.
Devouring blight had settled on her cheek,
And in the hectic flush had left a tinge
Of withering paleness in the eve of life:
In place of sunshine clouds assemble round,
Dark'ning with shadows the dull life of man:
The expiring spark of life at length dies out,
And leaves us mourning in the vale of tears.
Unconscious of all danger, her glazed eyes
Gazed upon vacancy and rigid grew;
And breathless were her lips, and dumb the voice,
When the immortal soul came issuing through
With a death-rattle from the stifled throat.
We lingering sigh and take a parting look
Of her cold marble relics in the shell,

With unfeign'd sorrow and repeated kiss,
Pausing upon the goodness of her heart
And the example of a well spent life,
Praying to God the Father to receive
Her angel spirit in the realms of bliss.

We know a change soon follows after death,
And that the air we breathe will grow impure;
But who could face the progress of decay,
Or look upon a hideous skeleton
After a while, when flesh dissolves away,
And nought but bones are left of our remains?

Removed to yon still city of the dead,
We pay our pilgrim visits to the tomb,
In fond remembrance of our dear beloved,
And linger round the spot that hides her dust,
While her bright spirit, peering through the sky,
Beholds the mourner on his bended knees,
Holding communion with the hallow'd corpse.
Some feeling heart has strewn her grave with flowers
Which shed a grateful perfume through the air:
The monuments inscribed tell who lies here,
And wreaths immortal show their love sincere.

Those we once knew we hope to meet again,
If not in mortal guise of earthly mould,

Yet in the spirit and familiar face.

Are we immortal ?—we lay down to rest,

And in oblivious slumbers soon forget

The past of being in the dreams of night,

Shrouded in darkness and the pall of death ;

But with returning sunrise wake again

To active scenes upon the stage of life,

Until we sleep the final sleep of all !

SONNET.

ADIEU TO THE MUSE.

———

LONG have we been acquainted, and to part
   From those we love breeds madness in the brain,
   And from the eye distilleth showers of rain ;
Each beating pulse of life surprised will start,
And ruin seize the desolated heart :
   We've travelled life together, — plough'd the
      main,—
   Search'd earth and heaven, and visited the slain :
The passions pictured, and the world apart
   Contemplated ;—the solitary cell,—
The mouldering ruins, and the gentle kind,
Have all been imaged by thee in my mind !
   In desert, or in dungeon I could dwell
If thou wouldst bear me company ;—my soul,
My life, I yield to thy divine control !

THE END.

www.ingramcontent.com/pod-product-compliance
Lightning Source LLC
Chambersburg PA
CBHW031346070726
47496CB00017B/1795